SECRETS

Hoping to put her secret sorrow behind her, Dr Edwina Gorton accepts the offer of working as a locum in a small town in Australia. However, she soon has reason to ask questions about the outwardly pleasant community: could the enigmatic chairman of the hospital board, Drew Collville, be hiding something? Is there a connection to the mysterious shed Edwina stumbled upon, deep in the State Forest? And can she keep yet another secret — her love for him?

ZELMA FALKINER

SECRETS

Complete and Unabridged

LINFORD
Leicester

First published in Great Britain in 2007

First Linford Edition
published 2009

British Library CIP Data

Falkiner, Zelma.
   Secrets - - (Linford romance library)
   1. Substitute physicians- -Australia- -Fiction.
   2. Women physicians- -Australia- -Fiction.
   3. City and town life- -Australia- -Fiction.
   4. Love stories. 5. Large type books.
   I. Title II. Series
   823.9′2–dc22

   ISBN 978–1–84782–754–8

Published by
F. A. Thorpe (Publishing)
Anstey, Leicestershire

Set by Words & Graphics Ltd.
Anstey, Leicestershire
Printed and bound in Great Britain by
T. J. International Ltd., Padstow, Cornwall

This book is printed on acid-free paper

1

The announcement broke into her cramped, half-awake, half-asleep world. 'If there is a doctor on the aircraft could they please indicate their presence to the flight attendants.'

Edwina took off her headphones, shoved them into the pouch on the back of the seat in front of her, and released her seat-belt. She stood up and reached for her medical bag in the overhead locker.

The chief steward hurried forward, checking the seat number against the names on the passenger list in his hand. 'Doctor . . . er, Gorton? A passenger in business class is unwell. Would you be prepared to give assistance?'

The wording of this question surprised Edwina. 'Prepared? Of course, I would.'

'Some doctors aren't.' He turned

back towards the front of the plane and, with a wave of his hand, indicated she should lead the way.

'They fear being involved in the paperwork of insurance claims, or worst still, litigation,' he went on, by way of explanation.

Edwina smiled. 'I suppose I'm still young enough not to be so cynical,' she said. And lacking experience in these matters, she could have added. This was her first long-haul, international flight.

They reached the curtain that divided economy and business classes. A flight attendant held it back to allow them through.

The patient was an elderly man with a complexion spider-webbed with the capillaries usually indicative of a heavy drinker of spirits. Sprawled across the extra-wide seat, he was breathing noisily, mouth agape.

Edwina loosened his tie and un-buttoned his shirt. As she put her stethoscope to his chest, her arm was clutched by an agitated woman presumably travelling with him.

'It's not DVT, is it, Doctor?'

'DVT? What makes you ask that? Has he a history of blood clots?'

'No.'

'Recent surgery?'

'No. It's just that back home there's been a lot in the papers about Australians suffering from DVT on the long plane trips to London and back.'

'I can assure you Deep Vein Thrombosis is not the problem with . . . is he your husband?'

The woman nodded. Edwina managed to disengage herself and listen to the patient's heart. It was steady and strong. So was his breath. She tried not to recoil from its whisky sourness.

'My opinion is he's probably been overdoing the sight-seeing,' she said diplomatically. 'How long have you been on holiday?'

'A month. Not all in England. We went across to the Continent as well . . .' The woman's voice faltered.

'Are you feeling all right?'

'Just tired,' the woman replied.

Edwina returned her stethoscope to her bag and snapped it closed. 'That's a lot of travelling to fit into one month. You both could possibly do with a good sleep. Don't worry, try and rest.' Patting the woman's shoulder, she moved past her to consult with the chief steward.

'Have you been serving him much alcohol?' she asked quietly.

'I understand he has been . . . well, demanding.'

'As I thought. That's what's wrong with him — he has over-imbibed. I suggest he be off-loaded at Singapore to do his snoring in a hotel room. Just to cover the airline.'

The chief steward pretended he was shocked. 'Sleep in Singapore! It's a shoppers' paradise!' he scanned his passenger list again. 'I see you are not having a stopover there. That's a pity.'

'Well, perhaps next time,' Edwina replied. If there ever was a next time, she thought.

Shopping stopovers were for people with more money than her, who didn't have to get a job quickly.

'Doctor, in appreciation of your help, I'd like to offer you a seat here in business class for the rest of the journey. Would you come this way, please?'

Edwina hesitated and looked back towards economy class. 'My cabin bag . . . and my book?'

'I'll bring them.'

Oh, what bliss! She'd be able to stretch her long legs. Just for diagnosing a case of drunkenness. It was amazing. Would that all her consultations turned out to be so easy — and so rewarding.

She thought of the clinic back in London with its steady stream of chronic cases. And the economy-class wages she was paid to work there.

She sank gratefully into the vacant seat. Beside her another passenger lay quietly under a sleeping-mask, the light-weight airline blanket tucked high around his shoulders. A quick glance told her this man was not going to be any trouble; a half-empty bottle of mineral water stood within reach of one uncovered, sun-tanned hand.

The destination map on the flight information screen showed her there were four more hours to Singapore. An undisturbed sleep now and a brisk walk around the terminal building before the last leg of the journey to Australia began would help with the jet-lag. And possible DVT.

Edwina eased her seat back into the reclining position and closed her eyes.

The lights and increased activity in the cabin woke Edwina. And the feeling that someone was staring at her. She sat up abruptly, momentarily confused.

'We're preparing to land in Singapore. You slept through breakfast.'

The speaker was the passenger in the seat next to her. The sleeping-mask no longer covered the grey-green eyes showing such an interest in her. She returned their gaze. How did he manage to look so immaculate she wondered.

Conscious of her own dishevelled state, she put up a hand to smooth her hair, and ran her tongue over her furry teeth. Great! She groaned inwardly. It was too late to freshen up; the fasten-seat-belts sign was on.

'This is just to drop-off and pick-up passengers and re-fuel so you'll have an hour in the terminal,' he added. 'That is, unless you're getting off here.'

It was an unspoken question, Edwina decided, but still she hesitated. Would it encourage him? The last thing she wanted was a man showing an interest in her; she was through with men, even handsome ones.

'No, I'm not,' she replied reluctantly.

'Good.'

The chief steward had appeared at her side. 'We'll have a wheel-chair ready for your patient when we reach the terminal, Doctor.'

Edwina saw her companion's interest in her go up a notch and sighed. It didn't say much for the man that he was impressed by her title.

7

Grateful for the interruption, she accepted her bag from the chief steward and moved to check on her patient.

There was no chance for further conversation when she returned to her seat. The aircraft landed and, in the bustle of disembarking, she lost sight of the man from the seat next to hers.

But she knew it was only postponing the inevitable. Unfortunately, the long haul from Singapore to Australia would give him plenty of opportunities to try and ingratiate himself. Good-looking men like him always seemed to. It was as if every woman was a challenge to them. Well, she told herself, she would just have to be ready for him, wouldn't she?

To her surprise, Edwina had to admit she was wrong; she didn't need to be on guard. Her companion was in no hurry to pursue the conversation when the flight resumed. The flight attendants had completed their routine of hot towels, drinks and refreshments before he turned to her.

'The chief steward tells me that you answered his emergency call.'

She nodded cautiously.

'Not many doctors would.'

'So I'm told.' Her indignation rose and overcame her reluctance to talk to him. 'I think that's terrible. We are doctors first and foremost.'

He threw back his head and laughed, showing strong teeth stark-white against sun-tanned skin. 'I love your enthusiasm.'

A hot flush suffused Edwina's face. 'There is no need to be patronising.'

He was quick with his apology. 'I'm sorry, I don't mean to be, but it is refreshing to meet someone so passionate about their calling. I'm Drew Colville, by the way.' He held out his hand.

She took it. 'Edwina Gorton.'

'And?'

It seemed churlish of her not to answer. 'I'm off to Australia for a three-month break.'

'A holiday?'

9

'I wish! No, I'll be looking for work. There are sure to be relieving positions available. At least, I'm hoping so.'

Drew Colville leaned forward. 'Tell me about yourself.' Although the words could be misconstrued, there was nothing flirtatious about his attitude.

Just as seriously, Edwina replied, 'Since graduating I've been working in a clinic in East London, and . . . I feel like a . . . break.' She stopped.

This man was a stranger and she wasn't about to confide her life story. How could she tell him she'd handled the relentless cycle of poverty and illness at the clinic, but that the heartbreak of her brother Timothy's slide into schizophrenia had torn her apart? When he committed suicide her need to get a new perspective on life took hold. A change of scene seemed the only way.

A familiar black cloud of sadness threatened. Determinedly, she warded if off. 'And what do you do?' she asked brightly. Apart from try to chat up women, she could've added.

'Among other things, I'm the chairman of the board of management of a hospital in a country town in Australia.'

Edwina couldn't believe her luck! 'Oh, we're in the same business! Tell me, will I have trouble getting locum work?'

He answered her with a question. 'Are you prepared to go anywhere?'

'Of course, but what exactly does that mean?'

'Not want to stay in the cities with the bright lights, traffic, regular hours . . . ?' he persisted.

Bright lights, traffic, regular hours? That was London. He couldn't know how much she wanted to leave all that behind her for a totally new experience. 'I'm expecting something different in Australia.'

'Do you have your credentials with you?'

'Of course.' Edwina leaned forward to reach into the cabin bag at her feet and brought out a plastic folder. She handed it to Drew Colville, confident he would find the contents more than satisfactory.

When he'd finished reading, he returned the folio without comment. 'How would you feel about general practice in a country town that has a hospital?' he asked.

'Well, that certainly would be a new experience but, why not? Am I likely to find such a job?'

Before he could answer, the flight attendants began preparing to serve a meal.

The conversation about the availability of work in Australia was resumed after the last of the meal had been cleared away and they were drinking their coffee.

'I have a friend, the only doctor in my town, who hasn't been away with his family for years,' Drew Colville said. 'Each summer he has to send them off to the seaside without him because doctors won't leave the cities, not even for a short spell of relieving.'

'Why doesn't the Government do something about that?'

'The Government has nothing to do with the running of the hospital. It's community-owned. That's why I can offer you the position. And how I can say Dr Bill would be very pleased to see you.'

Edwina could only stare at him. 'I hadn't expected it would be so easy,' she said at last.

'It must have been fate . . . '

'Fate?' A passenger who had too much to drink on a flight from London was fate? She couldn't buy that. 'Don't you mean chance?'

He airily waved a hand in the air. 'Fate or chance, whatever you like to call it, I'm not going to split hairs. The question is, would you be interested in taking a job relieving him?'

Edwina didn't know if there was something special about Drew Colville that made the offer seem so acceptable. Abandoning her usual cautious nature, and without asking any questions, she found herself nodding agreement.

There was no doubt he was pleased with her decision. 'Good, good,' he said, enthusiastically pumping her hand. 'So, it's a deal?'

'It's a deal,' agreed Edwina, her breath coming in a rush of excitement.

Later, when the cabin lights had been lowered and the other passengers settled down to snatch some sleep, the unasked questions surfaced. She realised she'd committed herself to work for a man she knew absolutely nothing about, in an unnamed town, she didn't know where, in a country she didn't know much about, all details she surely should have checked before agreeing.

Wide-awake, Edwina lay beside the sleeping form of her new boss, staring into the darkness.

What had she done?

2

For Edwina, the unreal, out-of-the-world feeling persisted through another day. As a doctor, she knew the reason was the rapid time-zone changes she'd been through had upset her body-clock.

Getting a hold on reality wasn't helped by the fact that everything about Australia was so different to the life she'd left behind. A city girl, she couldn't get over the vastness of the country.

They had been driving steadily since leaving the sprawling town on the banks of a broad, slow-moving river. Yesterday it had been the beautiful harbour city of Sydney, today, another flight and now this wide, brown land reaching as far into the distance as she could see.

The road stretched westward, tall trees meeting overhead to form a canopy that threw patterns of dappled light ahead of them. As the vehicle passed, flocks of pink-breasted birds wheeled in the updraught. Edwina gasped with pleasure.

'Galahs,' said Drew. 'You should see them at harvest time. They scavenge all over the road for grains from the wheat trucks. Wall-to-wall birds. Hard to miss them.'

'Where is everybody?' she asked. 'Except for the birds and the fields — '

Drew was amused. 'Almost there,' he laughed. 'We'll stop soon and have some lunch. With people.'

A tiny settlement came into view. They passed one or two houses fronting the road, then a wooden church standing alone. Its paint was peeling and the few crooked headstones under a lone pine made it seem even more forlorn.

A little farther on, Drew swung the estate-wagon off the road and parked. The building looked as if it had been sheltering beneath the huge tree for a long time.

Vehicles of all kinds, uniform only in their dusty, working state, clustered around the door, their haphazard parking giving them an air of abandonment.

Edwina's heart sank. This was the hospital? What had she let herself in for? Had she been downright foolish? She should've at least checked with the Australian Medical Association in Sydney.

'This is my local pub, The Gully,' announced Drew, coming around the vehicle to help her down. 'They serve great, what you English call bangers and mash.'

Edwina gave a weak laugh of relief. Bangers and mash? What could be more reassuring?

After the brilliance of the day, it was quite gloomy in the bar. A band of grizzled drinkers hailed Drew from a corner.

'I've brought you a doctor all the way from London,' he replied.

'An English doctor! Couldn't get an Australian to come, eh?' growled a voice from the back. 'They know too much, don't they?'

A frown creased Drew's forehead and was gone.

'She's too young and pretty to be a doctor,' joked another drinker, breaking the sudden silence.

'I've seen her papers, Jack, and she's a fair dinkum doctor, mate,' Drew responded.

Edwina declined the hotel-keeper's suggestion of a beer, aware of the ripple of comment from the group of men. Tea was produced and, at his call, two plates of food appeared, thrust by unseen hands through the strips of multi-coloured plastic guarding the doorway behind the bar.

The hot, sweet drink quenched her thirst, although she suspected it did nothing for her reputation.

'That'll stir the possums, as they say,' confirmed Drew in a low voice. 'The bush telegraph still operates out here, same as always. Satellites haven't changed that. By tonight, everyone will think of the new doctor as a teetotaller. Not the best start,' he teased.

'But I was thirsty,' protested Edwina, leaving aside the question of what the bush telegraph was.

'And hungry?'

She was. It had been an early morning start to get from their Sydney hotel to the airport, and the airline snack seemed a long time ago.

'We're miles from anywhere, how can this be your local pub?' she asked when her plate was empty.

'You'll have to re-think your idea of local,' he replied.

He didn't seem to think that needed explaining. It was some time before he realised she was waiting for answers to questions she couldn't ask. Not without sounding inquisitive about his private life, that was.

'My position as chairman of the hospital board is honorary,' he explained, somewhat reluctantly, she thought. It still didn't tell her much about himself.

'And you drive all this way . . . ?'

That made him laugh. 'All this way, as you put it, is not considered very far. Not to people in the Bush. You'll get used to it.'

Edwina couldn't imagine that, or what awaited her. When the dry, red-earth plains eventually gave way to scattered orchards and green plots on the outskirts of the town she was surprised by them.

'Irrigation,' offered Drew in answer to her unspoken question.

The rows of laden orange trees came right up to streets of well-tended gardens.

'It's delightful, like an oasis,' she exclaimed. 'I can't understand why doctors wouldn't want to come here to work.'

He gave her a sharp look. 'Who told you that?'

'You did, don't you remember? Then one of the men in the pub said something about Australians wouldn't come, that they knew too much.'

'Oh, that. He meant most doctors

prefer to work in the big city hospitals, as I told you. They know there'll be no nightlife out here.'

The surgery was a single-storey house in a pleasantly-shaded street in the centre of the town, close to the shops. A reception desk filled the hallway between the two main rooms. Behind them, a bathroom and well-equipped kitchen, and a small bedroom that opened off the enclosed back veranda.

The yard was empty of garden plants, but taken up by a rotary clothes-line, two or three bark-shedding trees and a late model Land Rover standing under a carport.

Although clearly this was not a family home, everything she'd seen so far was neat and clean, but different from anywhere she'd lived before. Just the place to begin the healing process, Edwina decided.

Her heart turned over with a familiar sadness at the thought of Timothy, but hardened and switched off as she remembered the changes his illness had brought to her life. That was still a no-go zone.

'The door wasn't locked,' she remarked to Drew after the tour of inspection.

'Nobody locks their doors around here.'

She couldn't believe it. 'What about security for the drugs?'

'Dr Bill only keeps the minimum and, except where they need refrigeration, they are in this cupboard. Trish, your receptionist, has the key. The really serious stuff is kept at the hospital. Most townspeople go there in an emergency. Don't worry. This isn't London. Everyone knows there's nothing to be gained by breaking in.'

Edwina still found that hard to believe, but decided not to pursue the matter for the moment. There were other questions she wanted to ask.

'How did you manage to arrange all this so quickly? I mean, the doctor and his family are gone already . . . '

'I e-mailed as soon as we landed in

Sydney. I imagine they couldn't get out of town quickly enough.'

Edwina raised her eyebrows at that.

'Before you changed your mind,' he explained. 'They've gone to Bali, so very little packing was needed. Just swimsuits.'

Drew turned to the reception-desk and flicked over the pages of the appointments book. 'I see there's plenty for you to do on your first day.'

'Good,' Edwina replied absently, her mind back on the unlocked door. Could she live here on her own? In a strange, Australian town in the middle of nowhere? He must think she'd be safe, or he wouldn't be leaving her here.

Something made her stop right there. How could she be sure of that? She knew very little, in fact, nothing about Drew Colville, but she'd followed him to what seemed to be the back of beyond, all on a chance meeting.

'You'll find plenty of food in the fridge, Trish would've seen to that. I'll be here on Monday at eleven, after

23

morning surgery, to take you on your hospital rounds. See you then, Doctor,' said Drew with a farewell gesture.

As soon as he was out of sight she turned and began a search for the house keys.

Edwina heard the front door open as she was washing her breakfast dishes. A ready explanation was that it was the receptionist, Trish. She dried her hands and went through to the hallway. It was empty, but the sound of faint rustling drew her into the waiting-room.

An elderly woman, her slight body twisted by arthritis, was tidying the magazines with knotted hands, and straightening the cushions to her satisfaction.

Edwina was disconcerted. Was this her receptionist? Another of Drew Colville's chance-meeting strays? There was so much she didn't know about the practice that she was going to need someone competent.

She controlled the dismay in her voice and said hello.

The woman turned carefully on her walking stick and said, 'You must be the English doctor.'

'Yes, I'm Doctor Gorton. Are you Trish?'

A snort dismissed the idea as ridiculous. 'No! I'm Myrtle Thompson.' A slow and obvious painful journey to the consulting room began.

Relieved but puzzled, Edwina followed. She was sure she'd locked the front door and back doors last night — and the night before that. 'How did you get in?'

'Oh, Trish showed me where the spare key was left, just in case the door was ever locked if I got here early. It never has been before so that's how I knew you'd arrived.' She gave an old woman's cackle. 'Only city-types worry about locking doors.'

Edwina ignored the last remark. 'The spare key?'

'Yes, she's probably told everyone where it is.'

Edwina decided she would not sleep

soundly again until the spare key was retrieved. But that depended on the missing Trish. She couldn't very well ask the patient. Actually, everything depended on Trish. Where was she?

As if she knew what was going through Edwina's mind, Myrtle went on. 'Sometimes Trish is late getting here . . . well, she often is. Can't seem to get herself organised. It's all that gadding about she does — she's no good in the morning.'

Something about the determined bent body warned Edwina not to do more than hold open the door to the doctor's room. She busied herself at the computer until Myrtle was seated, and her mind absorbing the information she had been given.

The computer screen flashed a request. *Password?*

Frustrated, Edwina swivelled her chair around to face her patient.

'Because I don't have the details of your file as yet, you'll have to tell me about yourself . . . ' she began, waving a helpless hand towards the computer.

'There isn't a file,' obliged Myrtle. 'Doctor Bill doesn't use one.'

'No file? I'll treat you as a new patient, then. How can I help you?' Edwina got out of her chair and began her questioning whilst wrapping the blood-pressure cuff around the patient's thin upper arm.

She could hear footsteps in the hallway and hoped it was the missing Trish, not more patients. She couldn't go on like this, the patient histories hidden in a computer that was password protected. She scribbled Myrtle's reading on a sheet of paper.

'Now, tell me, what can I do for you?'

'Nothing, Doctor. I just came to say hello.'

'That was very kind of you . . . '

'I come every Monday. Don't usually get my blood pressure taken, though.'

Her message delivered, Myrtle struggled out of the chair and shuffled towards the door.

'Are you on medication?' Edwina

asked, feeling guilty about under-servicing a patient. 'There are new drugs coming on the market all the time.'

The sudden about-turn took a lot of effort, painful effort judging by the grimace that twisted the old woman's face.

'Drugs? What's that about drugs?' she demanded fiercely.

Edwina was astonished by the response to her question. It had been a perfectly normal one between doctor and a new patient, but Myrtle obviously had taken exception to it.

Suddenly the door behind her flew open and the room was filled by a whirlwind personality.

'Hello, Myrtle!' carolled the new-comer.

'Hello yourself. You're late! Been out on the town again, eh?' All trace of displeasure was gone from Myrtle's face.

'Some people get lucky, don't they? The barbecue out at Weatherly went on and on. All night.' The younger woman moved to stand close to the patient and peer into her face. 'You wouldn't be jealous, by any chance, would you, Myrtle?' she teased.

There was a familiar snort from Myrtle, but Edwina could see she was pleased with the suggestion. 'Been there, done that,' she retorted scornfully as she negotiated the doorway. 'You young people think you invented a good time,' she added as she disappeared.

Still laughing, the younger woman turned to Edwina with an outstretched hand. 'I'm Trish.' She swung around and moved quickly across the hallway to survey the waiting-room before disappearing in the direction of the kitchen.

'Just time for a caffeine fix,' she called over her shoulder.

Despite her chagrin at the lack of an apology, Edwina found herself smiling as she followed her. There was something decidedly likeable about her receptionist.

'I haven't been able to access the patents' records without the password,' she said, stating the obvious.

The electric kettle whistled. 'Coffee?' asked Trish, reaching for mugs.

Edwina nodded. 'Is there any reason for Myrtle Thompson to have an appointment every week? She said she came in today just to say hello. I can't charge a consultation fee for that.'

Trish held up the milk carton and raised her eyebrows for the go-ahead before pouring some into Edwina's mug.

'Dr Bill doesn't.'

'She reacted very strongly when I asked her about drugs.'

There was a sudden stillness about the receptionist. 'You asked her about drugs?'

'Yes, I needed to know if and what medication she was on.'

'Oh, medication.' The lithe body relaxed.

'Yes. Because I couldn't access a file, I was completely in the dark as to the treatment for her arthritis,' Edwina explained.

'Of course you were,' Trish said, leading the way out of the kitchen. 'I'll show you how to get into the files, but I think you'll find Myrtle doesn't take any medication. Dead against it. Because of that, Dr Bill figures the best he can do for her is to let her make the effort to get herself here each Monday morning for a social visit. He says it keeps her out of the geriatric ward for a little longer.'

Edwina supposed that explained the old woman's strong reaction to her question about drugs. She shouldn't have been surprised; some people had decided views on the subject.

Trish tweaked the floral arrangement on her desk and went on. 'You can see she enjoys coming in and letting me know she's keeping tabs on my love-life.'

Edwina laughed. 'Well, we'll have to hope your love-life remains sufficiently interesting so we can watch over her, won't we?'

'Oh, it will. I can promise you that.'

3

Edwina lay in bed gazing at the patches of early morning light decorating the ceiling. It was another sunny day, but something about this one felt different. She looked at the bedside clock. There was a good hour before the alarm was set to wake her.

As she stretched to turn it off she realised that, for the first time in months, her awakening was not over-shadowed by melancholy.

She thought fondly of her brother. How Tim would've loved Australia, its warmth and its light. On their last holiday together he had revelled in the sunshine of the Costa del Sol. She smiled at the memory. And was surprised.

Could it be that distance had already given her a new perspective? Did that mean it was safe to revisit other painful memories? Such as matters of the heart.

Tentatively, Edwina allowed herself to think of Simon, expecting the usual rush of rage and hurt. None came. Emboldened, she said his name aloud. Even that failed to stir adverse feelings; it was just another name. Did that mean she was getting over him?

She had been devastated when Simon told her their relationship was to end; she couldn't believe he would desert her when she needed him most.

'It's just that Mother and Father think now Timothy has been diagnosed as schizophrenic . . . ' he'd begun.

Stung by the implication, she rounded on him. 'You're not going to tell me your parents believe it's in the family, are you? And do you think that, too?'

He stood miserably silent. She had her answer.

Her decision to get right away from familiar surroundings, and all that hurt, had obviously been a good one. As well, this locum-tenens in country Australia was a welcome change from London's winter gloom.

Settling into the practice had been easier than she expected and now, after two weeks in the town, she was feeling comfortable with her patients.

The sound of urgent footsteps in the hallway surprised her. Had she drifted off again and, with the alarm switched off, overslept? She glanced at the clock. It was still early.

'Edwina! Edwina!' Trish's call was anguished.

Edwina grabbed her robe and struggled into it as she crossed the room and out into the kitchen. 'What is it?'

She hardly recognised the distraught woman as her receptionist. Trish's hair, usually a riot of vivid curls, had been dragged back into a pony-tail to reveal a haggard face devoid of make-up. In her arms she carried the limp body of her pre-school-age daughter.

'Into the consulting room,' Edwina ordered, still buttoning her robe as she led the way. She checked the child's vital signs, her misgivings growing. This was not a simple childhood illness. 'Trish, when did you first notice she was feverish?'

'She was all right when Mum picked her up at the childcare — '

'Childcare? How many children attend the centre?'

'Fifteen or twenty, I don't know exactly . . . ' She lifted tear-filled eyes to Edwina. 'What is it? What's wrong with Melanie?'

'I don't know, Trish,' Edwina replied, reluctant to name her fears. She reached out and patted the mother's shoulder. 'You did well to bring her in so promptly.'

'She's all I have,' Trish said simply, snatching up the little figure off the examination table and holding her tightly against her chest.

It took no time for Edwina to throw on a track-suit and bundle Trish and her child into the Land Rover. Little was said between them during the short drive to the hospital, the usually exuberant receptionist giving only brief answers to Edwina's gentle probing.

A familiar yet unfamiliar figure strode down the hospital corridor to meet them. Edwina wondered what Drew was doing there at this hour. How had he learned of the potential crisis? It didn't matter, she told herself, he was there.

She had hardly noticed him as a man before, but now his very masculinity brought an air of reliability to the scene. Some of her anxiety disappeared; she wasn't alone.

Her relief was short-lived, overtaken by surprise when Drew went straight to Trish. He threw an arm around her shoulder and fell into step with her as they hurried behind the trolley.

Drew and Trish? Were they a couple? It was possible. The questions diverted Edwina momentarily from the sick child. She'd never thought of the private lives of either her receptionist or Drew Colville.

'What do you think, Edwina?' Drew

asked, breaking across her thoughts. The concern on his face raised another question in her mind. Was he the child's father?

'I fear it is meningococcal and it's unlikely to be an isolated case. We'll have to contact all the parents and vaccinate the children as soon as possible. There's a time factor involved here.'

'Leave that to me.'

It was afternoon before the back-log in the makeshift waiting-room was cleared and Edwina and Drew had a chance for a cup of tea with the Director of Nursing in her office.

The moment of relaxation didn't last long. There was a knock on the door.

Hastily Edwina took her stockinged-feet off the wastepaper basket and tucked them out of sight under her chair, straightening up as the health officer entered.

'Sorry to disturb you, Mrs Sweeny,' he said, addressing his remarks to the director of nursing. 'There's a problem.

It appears one of the mothers refuses to come in. She has a thing against immunisation of children.'

'But doesn't she realise what a dangerous, possibly fatal, disease this is?' asked Edwina.

'Yes, I've pointed that out to her, but it makes no difference. It seems the child hasn't had the usual schedule of shots, either,' the man replied.

Edwina looked at the director of nursing. 'She'll have to be persuaded.'

'I'll go,' offered Drew, getting up out of his chair.

'Thank you, but no. She'll be more likely to take notice of a doctor, and a woman doctor at that. And there's no reason why I can't go. Melanie is on six-hourly intravenous. I expect she'll recover fairly quickly.'

'But you must be exhausted,' protested Drew.

She shrugged. 'Aren't we all?' She turned to the health officer. 'Is her child ill?'

'I have no idea,' he replied.

'With that attitude, let's hope not. But I'll need directions. Will you write them down for me, please?'

It had been dark for hours when Edwina nosed the Land Rover into the carport and turned off the engine with a shaking hand. Only now that she was back safely could she admit to the fear kept dammed up behind a wall of denial.

With the isolation of the countryside fraying her nerves, the long drive in total darkness except for the headlights had been an ordeal she wouldn't want to repeat.

In fact, the whole day had been a horror. The responsibility of the diagnosis and keeping her head in the face of panicky parents would have been enough without the last few hours.

But it was over. I could kill for a long soak in a hot bath, Edwina thought. She gathered up her bag and swung her long legs out of the vehicle.

A shadow moved down the side of the house and became the figure of a man silhouetted against the faint glow from the street light. It startled her.

'Drew! What are you doing here?'

'Where have you been?'

The demanding tone of the question surprised her. He was almost shouting.

'You know where,' she replied.

'Yes, but that should have been home hours ago.'

Tiredness was threatening to overwhelm her.

'I don't want to talk about it right now.'

'Did you persuade the mother?'

Exhaustion made her impatient. What part of not now didn't he understand? she was tempted to ask, but he was her boss 'Yes, I did, but as I said, I don't want to talk about it. Tomorrow, Drew.'

'I was concerned about you.'

'Thank you for your concern. That must be a first.'

Even in the half-light, Edwina could see Drew's face change. She sighed. Why had she said that? A confrontation was the last thing she needed.

'Goodnight, Drew,' she said in a firm voice, putting an end to the conversation by scurrying into the house through the back door. Locking it behind her, she made straight for the bathroom, undoing her clothes and throwing them in the laundry basket as she passed.

The hot water gushed into the old-fashioned free-standing bath with a satisfying sound. While it was filling, she gathered her pyjamas and robe from the bedroom and carried them into the bathroom, pouring herself a white wine on the way through.

The room was filled with steam, just the way she liked it.

The tension of the day began to leave her body almost immediately. She took a sip of wine before sliding even farther into the water until it lapped about her ears, soaking the tendrils of hair that had escaped restraint, the bubbles tickling her chin. Blissfully, she closed her eyes.

A furious banging on the front door disturbed the peace.

Edwina sat up with a start that sent a wave of scented water over the end of the bath and out on to the floor with a resounding whoosh. Dismayed, she watched as a tide of foam spread toward the door.

The hammering on the door continued.

Reluctantly she stepped out of the depleted bath and reached for a towel for a hasty rub-down, wondering what new emergency needed her attention. And why they hadn't gone direct to the hospital as was usual.

'Coming,' she called as she struggled into her robe and padded across the kitchen with still-wet feet.

'Why is the door locked?' demanded her boss.

'Oh, it's only you, Drew,' she commented drily.

'The door was locked.'

Not liking the idea of anyone and everyone being able to wander in at will, such as now when she was in the bath, had been a good enough reason for Edwina to find a new hiding place for the spare key, known only to Myrtle.

'Yes,' she replied.

'Nobody locks their doors.'

Edwina clutched at the neckline of her robe. 'Well, this nobody does,' she retorted sharply.

Since this was obviously not a patient emergency, there was a chance she could return to her leisurely soak. That was, if she could get rid of him quickly. And, that was, if she hadn't used all the hot water. Water! Reminded of the mess his arrival had caused, she added mopping up to the list.

'What did you mean when you said that this must be a first,' he asked.

Edwina was lost. 'Pardon?'

'I was concerned for your safety and you said that must be a first. What did you mean?'

She exploded. 'Are you telling me you got me out of the bath just to ask that?'

* * *

Refreshed by an untroubled sleep, Edwina was beginning to see the events of the previous evening as an adventure. She was quite happy to share it with Drew when he invited her into the hospital board room at the end of rounds.

'I've ordered sandwiches,' he said, rather stiffly she thought. Whatever was bothering him was all very strange. Surely it wasn't her perfectly understandable outburst at being disturbed in her bath.

But even his formality couldn't curb her good spirits. Yesterday, she had contained a potentially-dangerous situation by quick diagnosis and action. And found her way home safely after being lost. Both confidence-boosting happenings.

'Thank you.' She was smiling as she sat down. 'Would you believe, Myrtle Thompson took over as receptionist yesterday. In the emergency I forgot all about surgery hours, but Myrtle didn't. Somehow she heard about it and got herself down there and did a great job. She was there again this morning, but wasn't needed . . . '

Edwina stopped. Drew probably knew better than anyone that Melanie was improving and Trish was able to leave the child's bedside and report for work.

'It's the country way,' was all he said, his manner still distant.

She looked at him enquiringly. What was wrong with the man? The child was well out of danger? Was there something going on between he and Trish this morning that was making him cranky? She didn't want to know about his domestic life.

'You were going to tell me what happened last night,' he prompted.

'Oh, that. I lost my way. Must have missed a turning somewhere. I got on to what was an almost unmade road with no signposts. Then I ran out of fuel . . . '

She looked at Drew, expecting him to find it amusing, but his face remained serious.

'It was pretty careless, letting that happen. Didn't you check the gauge before you left?' he asked.

'Of course I did. It was low, but I expected there would be a service station . . . What I didn't know was how far out of town the Robertsons lived.'

He shook his head. Leaving his chair, he paced the room for a while before stopping in front of her. His manner took her back to her schooldays when she'd been called before the head teacher.

'Rule number one in the Bush — check your fuel. It's a long way between petrol-pumps.'

Edwina conceded he had a point, as she'd discovered, but before she could acknowledge it he went on with his questioning.

'So, how did you get over that problem? Did another motorist come along?'

'Actually, no. By then it wasn't a proper road. I had to go looking for help.' A sudden memory of the rough and lonely track, the startled faces of the men as she trudged into the clearing among the dense trees, sent a cold shiver through her.

'Where on earth were you?' demanded Drew.

'I don't know. I told you, there were no signposts. I had to walk until I found this place — '

'What place? If it was a track then you were obviously in the State Forest. Was it by the river?'

'Well, it could've been. I didn't quite reach any river. The men there siphoned some fuel into a container for me — '

'You asked for a container of fuel?' Drew's voice was steadily rising but, engrossed in the telling, Edwina took no notice.

'Yes, and then I walked back to the Land Rover.'

It was only as she recounted the

events of that part of the day that she remembered there'd been something odd about the men's behaviour.

'That was strange . . . they didn't offer to drive me back to — '

He broke in. 'Don't you see what you've done? No, of course you don't. How could you? Let me explain. No-one, but no-one, goes wandering about in the forest and certainly not unaccompanied women. What did you see?'

'What do you mean? Are there wild animals in the forest?'

Drew threw up his arms in exasperation. Edwina became impatient.

'I don't understand all the questions. Why are you giving me the third degree? They supplied me with some fuel and told me I was on the wrong road, that it was a dead-end.'

'They were right, it's a dead-end. In the true sense of the word. More than you know. Tell me what you saw.'

'What I saw? Whatever are you talking about?'

Drew ran a hand distractedly through his hair. 'It's a simple enough question. What did you see?'

'There's no need for you to lose your temper, Drew.' Edwina reached for the last sandwich. 'I saw nothing.'

He raised a sceptical eyebrow at that. She tried harder to conjure up the scene in the forest. 'Just the usual farming things. Not a house, but a shed, one or two trucks . . . yes, two trucks,' she offered.

'A pump, pipes?'

'I really do not remember. I don't think so. I was tired because it had been an horrific day and I'd walked a long way . . . the sun was going down and there was still the problem of finding Mrs Robertson and changing her mind about vaccination.'

Edwina didn't want to admit how worried she'd been at the time; the forest had been quite threatening. 'I do wish you'd tell me what you're talking about. What was I supposed to have seen?'

Drew moved her empty plate aside and sat on the edge of the boardroom table, facing her, making a visible effort to question her more quietly.

'OK, so I can see you don't understand. How could you? But you must think carefully. Did you give the men your name? Tell them anything about yourself? They didn't see your vehicle, did they?'

Edwina was shaking her head now. 'No, no, no, the Land Rover was a long way back. I told you they were not at all talkative. Very surly, in fact, and rather frightening. It was all a bit scary.'

Something of her recalled fear must have reached him. He relented.

'I'm sorry. It's just possible you may have stumbled on a marijuana plantation.'

4

Only that morning Edwina thought the past was behind her and no longer had the power to affect her. How wrong she was! All her hatred of the people worldwide, who grew, harvested, and sold the drug, rose in her like gall, as bitter-tasting as ever.

Marijuana had robbed her of a beloved brother. The habit that began in Timothy's university days as purely recreational became addictive. She watched helplessly as his general health deteriorated and his behaviour. The hardest thing was that all her medical training was useless; as was common with the addicted, he didn't want to change. Or couldn't.

Finally, the irrational outbursts increased in frequency and he was beyond help.

'Edwina?' Drew's voice seemed to

reach her from a long way off.

She clamped down hard on her memories before they reached the inevitable outcome — the reliving of Timothy's death, with all its pain.

'Sorry. Surely you're joking, Drew.'

'I am not. We locals turn a blind eye, keep away from some reaches of the river. It's better not to become involved in these things.'

'I don't believe it!'

'Would you know what a marijuana plantation looks like if you saw one?'

'Well, no, Drew, I don't.'

'OK. Let's forget about it and hope they don't consider you a threat to them.'

'A threat to them? They were only farmers, weren't they?'

'They were growers.' There was a finality in his voice that was meant to warn her off, but Edwina couldn't let go.

'I can't believe this pleasant town is in any way connected with something illegal. It is illegal here in Australia, isn't it?'

'Yes, of course. Look, you'll have to take my word for it. Just don't go into the forest, or near the river without me, do you understand? Do I make myself clear?'

His dictatorial manner did not please Edwina. No-one had the right to speak to her that way.

'Do you mind?' she demanded in an icy voice.

Drew leaned forward and laid a hand lightly on her shoulder. 'It's for your safety. You don't realise how dangerous this could be,' he explained in conciliatory tones, 'if they came after you.'

Reminding herself Drew was her boss, she bit back a scornful retort and nodded agreement just to end the matter.

But it didn't. Later that day, in the cavernous supermarket, she felt a sudden uneasiness. She looked about her. The place was empty. Empty for the moment, that was, until three men appeared at one end of the aisle and advanced arrogantly, three-abreast, towards her. They were not looking at the goods on the shelves.

This is ridiculous, Edwina told herself. Drew, with his warning, has made me so nervous I'm looking for trouble. I'm in a supermarket, not out in the lonely Bush. She skipped around the corner into the next aisle.

That proved a mistake. The high shelves cut her off from the front of the store. She tried to put the brakes on her imagination with some commonsense, telling herself there must be a surveillance mirror. She swivelled her head. Somewhere . . .

There was none.

The expensively-dressed men appeared again. In the canyons of food products, their massive shoulders and unsmiling faces seemed more menacing than before. Her stomach lurched and the list of items fell from her useless fingers

Abandoning the shopping trolley, she hurried towards the checkout. The young girl there made no comment, staring vacantly into space as Edwina left the store empty-handed.

Out in the bright sunshine of the street, nothing had changed. Shoppers were going up and down, in and out of shops. She wondered what had happened to her. A grown woman being spooked in a supermarket was too ludicrous for words.

'Doctor!' The voice, right at her shoulder, made her jump. She swung around to see who was speaking and found she was hemmed in by the three men from the supermarket. Her throat tightened.

The speaker put out a hand that held a piece of paper. 'You dropped your shopping list,' he said.

The impassive face, masked by dark glasses, could have been carved from granite, it told her so little, but she accepted the gesture as friendly. She had to.

Somehow, she found a half-smile, took the proffered list and croaked her thanks.

Edwina grimaced at the first sip of

milk-less tea. She didn't like the taste at all, but black coffee would probably be worse. This was the price she had to pay for letting her imagination run wild in the supermarket, she told herself. There just hadn't been time to go back to the shops before evening surgery.

She still couldn't believe her reaction to the confrontation with the three men, it had been sheer panic. Anyone would think she wasn't used to men doing the shopping. But they weren't shopping, a tiny voice reminded her. She ignored it.

The men had a right to be there. And them knowing who she was wasn't the least bit surprising. She expected a stranger in town would excite comment, especially a new doctor.

It was all Drew's fault, she decided. He had made such a drama of her running out of fuel and filled her head with dark suspicions, some of which had stuck. No wonder she was nervous.

There was no way they could've been marijuana growers letting her know they knew who she was. She'd never seen the men before.

Relieved by the logic of that, Edwina turned her attention to the coming weekend.

From the kitchen window she could see the sun's last rays slanting through the line of clouds banked low in the western sky, turning them pink. What was the old saying? Red at night, shepherd's delight, red in the morning, shepherd's warning. Did that apply to this land down under?

If she'd remembered rightly, that meant the weather was going to be fine for the Rural Bush Fire Brigade's annual fundraising dance on an outlying sheep property. Edwina realised she was quite looking forward to it.

It seemed everyone she spoke with was going. Trish couldn't talk of anything else and it was the main topic of conversation at the hospital all week. The staff had included her in their party, promising her a good time with a real Australian flavour.

The two sales assistants in the town's only boutique were excited, too. They knew exactly what she should wear: their suggestion, a red sun-dress, hung in the wardrobe, together with a sturdy pair of sandals.

'The floor of the shearing-shed will be smooth enough, but getting up and down the steps could be tricky,' advised one. 'Especially down, at the end of the night.'

'Take your bag of tricks with you, Doctor. It might be needed,' added the other, joining in the laughter.

Edwina began to see what they found amusing when the car was parked in a paddock some distance from the shearing shed. Light sandals would have been hopeless on the rough ground.

The huge old building was high off the ground to allow shorn sheep to be sheltered underneath in bad weather, they told her. That meant there were wooden steps to be negotiated without the help of a handrail.

She was glad the sales assistants had

talked her out of her first choice of a long formal dress as well; that would have been impossible.

Inside, the party was well under way. Excited voices rose about the country-rock band, and revellers packed the area set aside for dancing. Edwina found there was no shortage of men to dance with. A stream of pleasant partners, anxious to meet the stranger in town, presented themselves.

She rested on a bale of hay during a band-break and took stock of the animated scene. Although it was well into the evening, Drew was nowhere to be seen. Above the heads, she glimpsed Trish at the far end of the shed, at the centre of a convivial crowd gathered around the bar. If they were an item, it seemed strange he wasn't there with her.

Edwina looked up with a smile and politely made room for a man to sit down beside her. Her goodwill faded as he flung an arm around her bare shoulders.

'Hello, Doc,' he leered, his fingers digging into her flesh. 'I've been waiting all evening for a chance to talk to you.'

Surprised by such familiarity she shrugged suggestively, but the hint was not enough to deter him. He was obviously not a man for such subtleties. In a more determined effort to shake him off without offending, Edwina stood up.

It was a mistake. Her tormentor rose with her, and without asking, gripped her forearm and pulled her in the direction of the dance floor just as the band started up again.

Although he wasn't drunk, Edwina didn't care for the man's effrontery. She still had the right to choose or refuse. With a decisive downward thrust of her arm, she broke his hold and took a step back.

'I'd really prefer not to dance this one, if you don't mind. Perhaps you could ask someone else,' she suggested, trying hard to disguise her distaste.

Whatever else he was, he was no fool,

recognising the rebuff. 'Think you're too good to dance with me because you're a doctor, do you? You English women are all the same, stuck up, noses in the air,' he shouted, pushing his face up close to hers.

The attack was so unexpected she could only stand astonished on the edge of the crowd. Despairingly, she looked about her for help, but the revellers seemed not to have noticed the outburst. Suddenly, she became aware of Drew thrusting his way through the dancers to put himself between her and the man.

'The lady's with me, Bluey, so buzz off,' he enunciated, leaving no room for doubt as to the result if Bluey didn't take the advice. To emphasise his meaning, his arm circled her waist and drew her close.

For a moment, Bluey defiantly resisted the warning, his chin thrust forward, but in the battle of wills, Drew proved the more convincing. Bluey got the message and disappeared.

Standing with Drew's arm still around her waist, Edwina wondered how many onlookers would notice and make something of it.

'You're shaking!' Drew exclaimed, looking down at her. He shepherded her through the crowd into a relatively quiet corner behind the wool-bins. 'Look, don't be alarmed by Bluey. He just thinks he's God's gift to women and comes on strong to anyone new in the district.'

Alarmed by Bluey? Edwina knew that wasn't her problem. He was just a man who wouldn't take no for an answer. Her problem was Drew's arm around her. His closeness in the semi-darkness was sending wild shivers through her that surprised her.

'I hope that isn't going to spoil your evening,' he went on.

Edwina found her voice. 'Of course not,' she said. 'Thank you for rescuing me. I seemed to forget my basic self-defence rules for a moment there.'

He grinned at her. 'Maybe your

self-defence rules aren't suitable for a ballroom, more for street fighting,' he suggested.

'Definitely not lady-like,' she admitted, grinning back at him. 'Definitely not. Very East London.' She had another thought. She looked around. 'Though I'd hardly call this shearing-shed a ballroom, so perhaps what I had in mind wouldn't have been out of place.'

He didn't take his laughing eyes off her. 'I should be offended. I think the shearing-shed looks very ballroomy with hay bales and the gum-tree branches around the walls doing a good job of overpowering the smell of sheep.'

'You brought that up, not me,' she teased. 'I never would've mentioned the smell. But I have to grant you, the place has a certain rustic charm.'

Standing beside Drew in the congenial atmosphere of the dance, conscious of his arm still around her waist, sharing a joke with him, the unpleasantness of a man who wouldn't take no for an answer was forgotten. The music pounded, Edwina realised she was enjoying herself.

She became aware of a stillness about Drew. As she turned a questioning face towards him, he withdrew his arm but didn't move away. Instead, he faced her and moved closer, placing a hand either side of her on the wall behind her, effectively encircling her.

Edwina's widening eyes watched as he slowly and deliberately bent his head, then paused only inches from her mouth, as if waiting permission to kiss her.

The shrill call of the compact mobile phone that hung around her neck broke the spell.

For Edwina, the interruption was welcome. She needed a moment to get her head together, to ask herself whatever was she thinking.

But what disturbed her most was a truth that had to be faced — she wanted Drew to kiss her. Like some love-starved teenager. It surprised her.

She searched her mind for an excuse.

Adolescent she may not be, but love-starved she could well be.

In the dark months after Simon's desertion, she'd vowed never to trust a man again.

She had succeeded — men became invisible to her. Until now.

This meant she wasn't just over Simon, she'd begun to have feelings again. That was good as long as those feelings weren't focused on any one man, she decided.

The mobile was insistent. She fumbled for it, her eyes still on Drew, and answered, glad yet regretful of the interruption.

'Edwina, it's Trish.'

'Trish! Where are you?'

'I'm in the bar. Have you seen Drew?' Without waiting for Edwina's reply, she went on. 'If you do, will you send him down this end?'

Edwina closed her phone. 'The wonders of modern technology. However did we manage before mobiles? Trish is looking for you down in the bar.'

'I'll take you home when you're ready,' Drew offered, without acknowledging the message.

Not sure she could trust herself, or him, being alone with Drew was the last thing Edwina wanted.

'There's no need for that, thank you, Drew,' she said hastily. 'I'll go with the guys. They probably won't want to stay much longer. I plan a busy day tomorrow . . . I mean today.'

★ ★ ★

Edwina pushed open the back door of the house and stepped inside. She kicked off her new sandals with a sigh of relief and padded across the verandah to the bedroom. Except for the episode with Drew, it had been a great night, but all she wanted now was to sleep.

She twisted one arm behind her to pull down the zipper of her dresser and stretched out the other to reach for the light-switch.

At first, she couldn't believe what she was seeing. The bedroom had been vandalised, the walls defaced with unintelligible scribbling, her few possessions thrown about the room.

Stunned, she went through the house, checking each room. The drugs cupboard had been forced open, its contents smashed, probably in anger because there wasn't anything of value to an addict in it.

The glass doors of the bookcase were shattered, the books strewn about the floor. Trish's reception area was a shambles, but strangely enough, the computer had been spared. Even the waiting room had received its share of attention from the vandals.

Edwina stood for a moment surveying the mess, wondering what to do next. It seemed pointless calling the police at this time of the morning; the damage had already been done.

In the silence of the night she could hear the sound of footsteps on the verandah. She stiffened. Had the vandals come back? Or never left? She looked about her for something to use as a weapon. There was nothing close at hand.

'Edwina?'

An hour ago she had not wanted to be alone with Drew, but now she welcomed his arrival. It wasn't the time to wonder what had brought him from the dance, just be thankful he'd come.

'I'm here, Drew,' she called, carefully picking her barefooted way across the room to open the door to him. 'I'm so pleased to see you. The place has been vandalised.'

His first concern was for her. 'Are you all right?' he asked, following that with more questions. 'Did you see them? You haven't called the police, have you?'

'Wait! Let me answer one thing at a time. I'm all right, I didn't see them and I haven't called the police. I didn't think there was much could be done in the middle of the night.' She looked around her. 'I'll do it later in the morning.'

'I don't think this is a police matter,' Drew said.

Edwina couldn't believe her ears. 'Isn't vandalism a crime in Australia?'

'Yes, but this isn't mindless vandalism — '

'Not mindless vandalism? What do you call it?'

'If it was mindless vandalism, the medical equipment would be damaged, too. But it isn't. No, I'd call it a warning.'

A cold hand clutched at Edwina's heart. 'From whom? What about?' she asked, suspecting she already knew the answers.

Drew crunched over the broken glass to the window and looked out into the darkness for a long moment before turning to answer her.

'I think it's a warning not to talk about what you saw in the forest.'

'But I saw nothing,' she protested.

'They obviously thought just finding them was enough.'

'If you're so sure I stumbled on a

marijuana plantation, isn't that all the more reason to report it to the police?' she asked.

'Edwina, listen to me. I know what I'm talking about. This is a warning. Take it and forget all about what you did or did not see. It's saying you're an outsider, and while you're here, don't rock the boat.'

It wasn't advice Edwina was prepared to accept without question. 'Granted, I'm an outsider, but are you willing to forget there's marijuana growing in your district, too?'

'I don't know that there is. I didn't see it, did I?'

She stared at him in amazement. Didn't he care? 'I could show you,' she asserted.

'Could you? Weren't you lost?'

'I could try and find the place again.'

Drew seemed to lose his patience at that. He strode through the debris and took her firmly by the shoulders.

'Edwina, leave it alone,' he begged.

She stared defiantly into his eyes, her

hated of marijuana making her deaf to his entreaty, unafraid of his displeasure.

He sighed and dropped his hands. 'Let's go over to the hospital and find somewhere for you to sleep,' he said. 'You can't stay here.'

5

Myrtle Thompson was quick to criticise the effort Edwina and Drew had put into cleaning up after the vandals.

'You didn't do a very good job, did you? Too much for one person. Should have got someone in to help you,' she pronounced as she settled in for her Monday morning visit.

'I did. Drew helped me,' Edwina said.

'Drew Colville? As good as useless,' Myrtle gave her characteristic snort. 'You'll need new cushions for the waiting room. I'll get the Country Women's Association to make some more.'

'Why, thank you. Now, have you thought any more about trying this herbal remedy to relieve your arthritis?'

'What did the police say?'

'They weren't notified.'

'Why not? It's vandalism, isn't it?'

'Drew decided — '

Myrtle snorted again.

'I'm under contract to the hospital and he is the chairman of the board,' Edwina pointed out.

Myrtle didn't look convinced by the explanation. 'All the more reason why the police should be notified. There's more to this than meets the eye, Doctor.' She fixed Edwina with her gaze. 'What's going on?'

Edwina could see the only way to satisfy Myrtle was to tell her the truth.

'Well, I became lost one day — the day of the meningococcal scare, and ran out of fuel . . . I walked to what I thought was a farm and asked for help. The men there gave me a can — '

'Where was this?'

'Myrtle, I was lost!'

'Was it in the forest?'

'As a matter of fact, that was what Drew asked me. I suppose it was. It was all Bush to me.'

'What did you see?'

'Whatever is the matter with you people?' Edwina joked. She could hear more patients arriving and knew persuading Myrtle to try something to relieve her symptoms would have to wait for another day. 'I really have to attend to — '

'What did you see?' Myrtle repeated.

'As I told Drew, I saw nothing untoward. Now, if you'll excuse me, I must get on.'

Myrtle struggled out of the chair and began to leave. At the door she turned and waved an arm towards the glassless bookcase, the forced drugs cupboard. 'And what does Mr Drew Colville think of this?'

'He thinks someone is warning me not to talk. He told me not to go to the police.'

Before Edwina could reach out, Myrtle's gnarled hand managed to twist the door-knob and open the door. The buzz of conversation from the waiting patients almost drowned her parting comment.

'Oh, well, he would, wouldn't he?'

The strange comment stayed with Edwina for the rest of the morning. Whatever did Myrtle mean? Annoyed with herself for not being able to put it out of her mind, she decided there was only one person could give her an answer.

★   ★   ★

It wasn't hard to find the neat little cottage in a back street. Myrtle was in the garden, a broad-brimmed hat shading her from the sun as she dead-headed the profusion of over-blown rose blooms. Edwina was impressed and said so, but Myrtle shrugged off the praise.

'Nothing to it. These are special secateurs. They don't need as much pressure,' she said, holding them up in her arthritic hand to demonstrate. 'There's nothing wrong with me, so I take it this is a social visit. Have you time for a cuppa, Doctor?'

'Yes, thank you,' answered Edwina,

following the old woman into the cottage.

When they were seated, Edwina asked the question that had been bothering her all day. 'What did you mean about Drew not wanting me to go to the police? Is there something I should know?'

Myrtle gave her a long, hard look. 'You'll be leaving soon, won't you?'

'Yes, at the end of the next week, when your Dr Bill comes back from his holiday.'

'That's why Drew Colville wouldn't want you to go to the police. You'd get involved in proceedings and not be able to leave.' She sank back in her special chair.

Of course. Feeling slightly foolish, Edwina asked herself why she hadn't thought of that? She could see it would be messy from the hospital's point of view, too.

But something about the remembered tone of Myrtle's cryptic comment gave the lie to that explanation. It had been . . . Edwina searched her memory. It had been . . . scornful.

'Myrtle, that makes sense, but I don't think it is what you meant.'

The old eyes seemed to cut right through her, almost defiantly. Edwina felt guilty for bothering Myrtle, but the hint of something sinister about Drew couldn't be ignored.

She decided to make a joke of it. 'You wouldn't want me to die wondering, would you?'

'Die?' The word was like a whip-crack. 'Why do you say that? What do you know?'

'It's just one of my mother's sayings,' Edwina protested, surprised at the response. 'She used to ask my brother and me when we were impatient to try something new if we were afraid we'd die wondering. As I keep telling Drew, I know nothing.' She leaned forward. 'But there is something you're hiding. About Drew.'

Feeling slightly ashamed, Edwina rose from the sofa. 'I'm sorry I bothered you, Myrtle. I know what my mother would say about that, too — she'd say I'm forgetting my manners, and I am. Thank you for the cup of tea.'

She stooped to take up the tea-tray and carried it to the tiny kitchen. 'Don't get up, I'll see myself out. See you next Monday.'

'Doctor!' Myrtle called as Edwina reached the door. She'd pressed the button on her Lifta-Chair and was standing. 'What do you know about Drew Colville? Have you ever asked yourself where he gets his money?'

Edwina thought it was quite ironic, really. She'd gone to Myrtle Thompson out of curiosity, to ask one simple question, and set in train a round of fruitless questions about Drew Colville.

★ ★ ★

As she walked to the surgery door with the last patient for the evening, the merry-go-round in her mind began

78

again. What did she know about Drew? Very little, she had to confess. And why did she need to know? The answer to that was she didn't.

She was leaving. Soon the town, and Drew, with his suspicions about marijuana plantations, would be part of her past.

Edwina smiled as she turned the key in the lock. It had been weeks, but she still hadn't overcome her unease at sleeping in an unlocked house.

Twin headlights flashed in the transom-window as a car pulled into the driveway. She sighed and turned the key again. Evening surgery was obviously not over.

But it wasn't a late patient who stepped on to the verandah as she opened the door.

'Drew!'

'Hello, Edwina. Surgery over? Good. Seems I've timed it just right, then.'

Edwina could feel her ears burning. He couldn't possibly know it, but this man had occupied her thoughts all day.

'Come in, Drew, I'm just about to make coffee. Would you like a cup?' She was pleased with how cool and collected she sounded.

He followed her into the kitchen. 'I doubt you're here as a patient,' she went on, knowing he wasn't. 'You look remarkably well.' And handsome, she had to admit, surprised at herself for noticing that.

'I am. No, my visit is of a more personal nature.'

Edwina raised her eyebrows.

'You're leaving us next week . . . '

She nodded.

'I . . . You have done a good job, fitted in really well . . . '

She nodded again, encouraging him.

Drew looked around the kitchen. 'Perhaps we could go . . . '

'Into the waiting room?' she prompted, leading the way. 'Myrtle's friends replaced the cushions,' she added.

'I . . . we . . . ' he began again. 'I wondered if I could take you to lunch

. . . by the river, one day before . . . '

To Edwina it seemed a perfectly normal thing for the chairman of the board to invite a departing colleague to a farewell lunch. She wondered why he was having so much trouble getting it out.

'I'd like that, thank you, Drew.'

'Good. Shall we say the day after tomorrow?'

★   ★   ★

The first patient could be heard crossing the hall to the waiting room next morning before Edwina had a chance to bring up the subject of her luncheon date with her receptionist.

'Oh, by the way, Trish, don't make any appointments for home visits or evening surgery tomorrow. I'm taking the afternoon off.'

Trish rinsed her coffee mug. 'And what will you be doing on your afternoon off?' she asked over her shoulder.

'Drew is taking me to lunch.'

Trish slammed the mug down on the draining board and swung around. 'Drew is taking you to lunch?'

Suddenly, Edwina was having as much trouble telling Trish about the lunch as Drew had had in asking. She became aware of the need to pick her way carefully through the minefield of her receptionist's feelings.

'Yes,' was all she could think of to say.

Trish's eyes narrowed and her voice became steely. 'And why is he taking you to lunch?'

'It's to thank me before I leave. I presume others will be there if it's official,' she explained. Even to her ears it sounded defensive. 'I have no idea where. He just said lunch by the river.'

Trish relaxed visibly. 'Oh, yes, by the river, that'll be Si Bella, the Italian restaurant. Very nice. The food's excellent and the wine cellar more than adequate.'

'Good. That's why I don't want any

patients waiting for me when I get back.'

Trish's laugh told Edwina the awkward moment had passed. But it didn't help with the other pressing problem — what did one wear to lunch by the river?

The two girls in the boutique welcomed her. 'Si Bella for lunch?' They hummed and haahed, and argued with each other amongst the racks. Edwina stood back, bemused by the flurry she'd caused.

The choice was finally narrowed down to a bias-cut slip dress of buttercup yellow silk that hugged her body as far as her knees. Teamed with a pair of strap sandals, it would be a smart casual outfit suitable later for her planned resort holiday on the Barrier Reef.

Later, Edwina was smoothing her dress over her hips when she heard Drew's vehicle. Thankful Trish had already left to pick up her daughter, she hurried out to meet him.

'Why, hello!' There was no mistaking

the admiration in his voice and eyes.

And there was nothing of the cool and collected doctor about her response. Forgetting Trish, Edwina spread out her arms and twirled in front of him.

'Is this a classic case of letting-the-dog-off-the-leash syndrome, Doctor?' he asked.

She laughed, her nervousness disappearing completely. 'Something like that,' she replied, allowing him to open the passenger-side car door for her. 'Let's go, Drew, I'm starving.'

He settled into the driver's seat. 'It's a bit of a way out,' he murmured apologetically, swinging the vehicle on to the street.

Edwina looked at her companion for the first time that day. Properly. He was not wearing his usual formal dark suit and tie. A lightweight sports coat was thrown over the back seat and the pale blue shirt, open at the neck, was of fine cotton, both obviously expensive. She had to concede that man had style as well as money.

Unbidden, Myrtle's parting remark sprang to mind, quickly quashed, together with her vague feelings of guilt. Both his source of income and his future were none of her business.

'Isn't this the way to The Gully?' she asked.

He flashed her a smile. 'Mmmmm.'

'Is Si Bella out this way, too?'

'Si Bella? He took his eyes off the road for a little longer this time.

'Aren't we going to Si Bella for lunch?'

He laughed. 'Now why would you think that?'

Indeed, why would she? Edwina realised Trish has assumed the venue would be Si Bella. Wrongly, as it happened. She looked down with dismay at her dress, bought with that same wrong idea in mind.

'It's just that Trish said . . . ' Her voice trailed off at the beginnings of a frown on Drew's face.

'You told Trish?'

'Why, yes, didn't you? I had to tell

her I was going out to lunch — '

'And I presume it was she who suggested Si Bella?'

Edwina wasn't going to admit how foolish she felt. 'Yes, probably because that's where you take all your dates.'

'Spot on, Edwina. But the difference here is you are not, one of what you call, my dates, are you?'

Something had gone out of the day. Edwina turned her face away and gazed silently out of the side window at the passing scenery — if the flat, dry landscape could be called scenery. They had left the green of the township behind.

Drew swung the vehicle off the bitumen on to a dirt road. She wanted to ask what kind of a restaurant would be this far from any habitation, but her hurt pride wouldn't let her. At least his local, The Gully pub, had a few houses around it. This road was bordered by paddocks — and sheep.

Before long they rattled over a stock-grid. In the distance Edwina could see a line of trees. Curiosity overcame her pique. She turned to Drew and raised an eyebrow.

'The river,' he explained.

Ah, lunch by the river was to be a picnic. Her heart sank. A picnic in high heels? Fleetingly, she wondered how did one get grass stains out of yellow silk? She twisted in her seat-belt to look in the back for a picnic rug and hamper. Nothing. Turning back she caught the faint smile on Drew's face. He was enjoying his surprise.

The trees were closer now. The vehicle clattered over another stock-grid, more ornate than the last, with stone pillars on either side.

A tasteful sign attached to one read, *Island Bend*.

Edwina could see out-buildings and then, at the end of a curved avenue of towering trees with creamy-grey trunks, the sprawling homestead.

Set in a large garden and surrounded on three sides by wide verandahs, it overlooked a stretch of the river and the bend that gave it its name.

Drew's smile widened into a grin. 'Lunch by the river as promised,' he said. 'With my parents.'

* * *

Edwina relaxed into the comfortable upholstery as the vehicle hummed its way through the blackness of the country night. Its headlights pierced the dark, occasionally reflecting bright eyes of nocturnal bush creatures by the roadside.

'What a lovely day, Drew. Thank you so much.'

He nodded acknowledgement. 'You really enjoyed yourself, didn't you?'

She half-turned in the seat. 'Yes. Your parents were charming. And following those wallabies into the forest, well, that was something else . . . it was magical seeing them bound off between the trees. It was good of you to show me.'

'From the back of a motor bike wasn't too much?'

'It was rather rough going,' Edwina admitted with a laugh, ruefully running her hands over her buttercup-yellow silk dress.

'It reminded me of . . . ' For a moment a sadness clouded her pleasure as she remembered exhilarating rides clinging behind her brother. 'It reminded me of someone . . . I once knew.'

'You never mention your past, Edwina.' Drew took his eyes off the road briefly to give her a questioning glance.

She hesitated, then replied. 'There isn't much to mention, actually.'

'Don't you have family?'

'Well, no. There was only the four of us. My dad died in a work-related accident early in my life, and shortly after I graduated, Mum died. It had been a struggle and I think she was tired.'

'You said there were four of you.'

'Yes, I had a brother, Timothy.'

'Had?' he probed gently.

'It's a sad story, that's why I don't talk about it.' Edwina blinked away a tear. 'I haven't fully accepted his loss.'

Drew reached out and covered her hands with one of his. It was a brief but comforting gesture. She was sorry when, with a little squeeze, he let go to put it back on the steering wheel.

'I shouldn't have asked, but I wanted to know more about you. I hope I haven't spoilt your day.'

'Nothing could spoil today.'

'Not even the wrong clothes?'

Edwina smiled at his attempt to lighten her mood and responded to it. She had to admit one thing was spoiled — the buttercup-yellow silk dress. It hadn't taken kindly to a motorbike ride into the forest.

'Don't think you're off the hook yet, Drew Colville,' she warned. 'You tricked me.'

The lights of the town were visible in the distance. Cocooned in the speeding vehicle, acutely aware of the man beside her, Edwina could feel the rapport between them growing. There was much more to him than she'd first thought, such understanding.

Drew's face was soft in the glow of the instrument panel. Suddenly, she wanted to tell him her secret.

'My brother was schizophrenic.'

6

The moment of silence lengthened into minutes. To Edwina, the cabin of the speeding vehicle suddenly seemed claustrophobic as the affinity between herself and Drew that had encouraged her to confide in him, evaporated.

The street lights, more frequent now as they drove into the centre of the town, illuminated his set face. She turned her head away, sick at heart. It had been a mistake to tell him — he was no different to Simon. He had baulked at the word schizophrenic.

Drew swung the estate-wagon in through the gateway to the surgery and brought it to a halt. He hurried to open the door to let her out, and escorted her to the front door.

In silence.

'Are you coming in for a coffee?' she asked woodenly, quite sure he would refuse.

His answer was as she expected, courteous and just as stiff.

'Well, thank you again for the day,' she said. The day of happiness that lay in ruins, she might have added.

Her throat tightened. She was sure she'd cry in front of him if he didn't leave soon.

'I'm glad you enjoyed it.'

Such politeness! Oh, why wouldn't he go? Quite desperate, she fumbled the door open, switched on the light and, with a hurried good-night, stepped inside.

Only then did she allow the tears to flow. All the hurt of the past came back to gnaw at her. She had lost a dearly loved brother to marijuana. Was it going to rob her of meaningful relationships for the rest of her life?

She woke next morning composed, but hollow-eyed, with no appetite for a proper breakfast.

The dull thump of a walking stick sounded on the wooden verandah. Edwina glanced at the kitchen clock. It was much too early for consultations. She gulped down the last of her orange juice and went to investigate.

'Myrtle! Are you all right? Whatever are you doing here? It's not your day.'

'I wanted to see you before you began surgery. I need to talk to you.'

'Don't tell me you've decided to take my advice and get a walking-frame after all. Or go on medication.' Edwina opened the door to the consulting room. 'Come on in.'

It took the old woman the usual long time to painfully settle in the chair. Moved by the struggle, Edwina repeated her advice.

'I do wish you'd let me prescribe something for you.'

Myrtle waved the suggestion aside impatiently. 'You went out with Drew Colville yesterday.'

Edwina knew she shouldn't be surprised. Not much passed unnoticed in a town this size. Though what it had to do with her patient she couldn't imagine.

94

She stifled the automatic retort about it being her own business.

'Yes, he wanted to thank me . . . before I left.'

'Where did you go? I'm told you were dressed up to the nines.'

'Si Bella,' Edwina replied, determined to keep to her story.

Myrtle snorted. 'Spending hospital money, I suppose.'

'Well, it was official hospital business.'

'Best you keep it that way. I like you — '

'Why, thank you, Myrtle. The feeling is reciprocated.'

'And because I do like you, I've come to warn you not to get tangled up with Drew Colville. He's bad news.'

If only you knew, there's no chance of me getting tangled up with Drew, as you put it, thought Edwina.

'Thank you for warning me. I'd already worked that out. Bit of a charmer, I suppose you mean.'

Myrtle leaned forward in the chair.

'That, too,' she conceded. 'But there was talk, during our bad times, that he and Detective Walsh were on very good terms. Very good terms.'

Despite herself, Edwina was intrigued. 'What do you mean by bad times?'

Myrtle was not about to be diverted. 'They were as thick as thieves. And lately he's been seen in his company again.'

Edwina decided no good would come of the conversation — it had to end.

'I appreciate the thought behind your visit, Myrtle,' she said, 'but it has nothing to do with me. Drew is my boss and I'm only interested in our work together at the hospital — '

'Ah, the hospital! Where did the money come from to set up the hospital when the Government opted out? You think about it, Doctor. I wasn't going to mention it when it was only work, but now you're getting involved with him — '

'Stop right there, Myrtle. I am not getting involved.' Edwina glanced at her watch and stood up, pushing her chair back, determined to have the last word.

'Now, promise me you'll think some more about that walking frame. It would make getting about so much easier, give you more support than a stick, and relieve the pain. Without medication.'

Myrtle wasn't about to let her get away with that. 'And you think about what I told you,' she said.

There was no need for Myrtle to admonish her. Edwina knew she would think about it, but not just now. It was time for Trish to arrive. She had to be faced. And lied to.

The old woman was out of the patient's chair and moving slowly towards the door, her face brightening.

'There's Trish! Have you noticed she's been a lot more reliable since she's not gadding about with Drew Colville? He's no good for her, either. And I told her so.'

'Thank you for coming in, Myrtle. You're right about Trish. She's here.'

'And I'm right about Drew Colville,' added Myrtle, winning the competition for the last word.

Edwina wasn't sure when the idea of going to the police came to her. Drew's reaction to her disclosure had opened old wounds.

And despite herself, Myrtle's insinuations coloured her thinking.

The vandalism of the surgery had been repaired, the new cushions made by Myrtle's friends bringing an air of normality to the waiting room. But the thought of a possible marijuana plantation going unreported nagged at Edwina. She decided something should be done about it.

Having made up her mind, she hurried through the morning, grabbed a sandwich to eat on the run and drove to the police station. The building, and the court house next to it, belonged to a more gracious era, but time, and most probably funding cuts, had not treated it well.

Inside, she found the station almost

deserted. 'It's quiet in here,' she remarked to the officer on duty behind the desk.

'The action is next door at the Magistrates' Court today,' he replied, hardly taking his eyes from the pile of documents he was sorting. 'What can I do for you?'

The man wasn't exactly indifferent, but Edwina could tell her complaint was not about to make his day. She had begun to explain when the front door swung open.

'Ah, there you are, PJ!' the officer greeted the newcomer with obvious relief. 'This young lady has a complaint about vandalism. I'm up to my neck in court records — they're needed right away. Would you attend to it?'

The grossly overweight man standing in the doorway registered little more than the minimum of official interest in Edwina.

'Come through, Miss.'

'Doctor!' she corrected icily, expecting it to make an impression on his insolence.

It didn't. Walking ahead of her, he led the way to an office and sat down. 'I'm Detective Sergeant Walsh, here for the Magistrates' Court.'

Was this extremely rude policeman linked to Drew as Myrtle implied? It didn't seem possible; Drew was too urbane to find such an uncouth man a good companion. Unless something other than friendship brought them together.

'And who might you be?'

'I'm Doctor Edwina Gorton.'

'And?'

'There's been some vandalism — '

'Where?' He interrupted to ask the question indifferently, head down, his pen poised over the form in front of him.

'At the surgery.'

Edwina had the detective's full attention at last. His head jerked up sharply, the unusually small eyes in their pockets of loose flesh alert and taking in the full length of her.

'And you are?'

'I told you.'

He looked back down at what he had written. 'Yes, but at the surgery, you say.'

'I'm acting as locum for Dr Bill — '

'Yes, yes. Vandalism, eh? We'll get in touch with Drew. Thank you for coming in.' He stood up.

Incensed, Edwina rose with him. 'Don't patronise me. I'm here to tell you about it. Drew thinks it's connected with — '

'They might let their women take care of these matters in your country, Doctor, but out here in the Bush, we men do all the dirty work for our women.'

She could not believe the menace in his voice, but refused to be intimidated by it.

'Perhaps you have a problem with women, Detective. Unfortunately, it was me, a woman, not Drew, who stumbled on to what may or may not be a marijuana plantation. I'm sure you'll want to know more about it. When

101

you're ready to question me, I'll be at either the surgery or the hospital.'

Twin fires of outrage burned in her cheeks, but Edwina managed to calmly turn at the office door with her own warning. 'I wouldn't leave it too long; I will be gone soon.'

She marched past the officer at the desk without acknowledging him and out on to the wide steps. Undecided as to her next move, she stood there surveying the main street.

Directly opposite was the office of the local newspaper. Just the people I need, she decided. They will love this story!

There was nothing patronising about the editor. Tall and thin and rather bookish looking, he introduced himself as Hugh White and let her voice her indignation without interruption.

'I'm sorry,' he said when the storm was over. 'I don't know how I can help you.'

'What rot! You can publish what I'm telling you. The police don't seem interested to hear I may have found a marijuana plantation, or that someone has vandalised the surgery. I think the townsfolk have a right to know that about their police force.'

'You must realise the paper can't make unsubstantiated accusations against the police every time someone thinks they have cause. We'd be in trouble if we did. No, I can't help you. The police are still the people you must deal with.'

'But I'm talking about illicit drugs here!'

'As I understand it, you don't even know where it was you stumbled on this alleged plantation.'

'Drew thinks I may have been in the State Forest.'

'The State Forest! Do you have any idea how many acres that covers? Thousands! All along the river.'

'A needle-in-the-haystack job, and definitely not one for a newspaper.'

'Sounds pretty slack to me. Surely newspapers have a responsibility to reflect community concern.'

'Yes, but you're missing the point. We

only have your complaint. That surprises you? Look, I think you should read our back issues. All on microfiche. I'll set it up for you.'

The ugly story shook her. It began with the secret planting of the district's first marijuana crops. Undetected among the vines and orchards under irrigation, they flourished. The newly-rich growers attracted attention to themselves by building lavish new homes, opening new businesses with laundered money. They became contemptuous of the law.

Edwina stopped reading with the sudden memory of the three men in the supermarket. Their dress and manner made sure they stood out.

She shivered and turned her attention back to the screen and continued reading.

The first of the police raids brought swift and ruthless revenge from the growers. Three unsolved murders followed as suspected but innocent informants were eliminated.

Eventually, the Government was

forced by public opinion to set up an enquiry, but no-one was brought to justice. The tentacles of the powerful empire had reached into and corrupted the police force at the highest level. Forewarned, the ring-leaders fled overseas.

But the town had already lost its innocence.

There was more, but Edwina had had enough. She switched off the reader, staying in the chair, staring at the darkened screen, unable to get up and leave. She felt quite sick. What was she up against?

She couldn't blame Hugh White. The editor had done the right thing in directing her to the archives. He knew she was blundering into something she didn't understand and that only facts would satisfy her.

From where she sat in the front office of the newspaper, she could see across the street to the police station. Was DS Walsh a corrupt policeman or just an ill-mannered woman-hater?

'Does Drew know you're here?' Hugh White's voice at her shoulder startled her. She swung the chair around, wondering at his question.

'Why, no.'

'I think you should hold your horses, Edwina. He might not be pleased with you going to the police.'

'I can't see what it has to do with him. My contract with the hospital makes no mention of my private life,' she said defiantly, knowing he was right.

'No, I meant he might be concerned for your safety. As you can see, these guys mean business.'

'Mean business? Weren't they put out of business?'

'There's always the chance they've started up again, or that there's a new generation of growers.'

Edwina shook her head in disbelief. 'I cannot get over you all accepting the situation.'

'As you've just read, we've been there, done that.'

'But don't you know what marijuana does to young lives?'

The editor put a hand on her shoulder. 'Better than most,' he said seriously. 'The best we can do is make sure our children know of its danger.'

Still deeply disturbed by what she'd learned of the town's dark secret, Edwina shook off his hand and got up. 'I'm glad you feel satisfied with that,' she retorted as she stalked out of the offices.

Trish seemed less than her usual bright self as she blew on what she called her pre-work heart-starter coffee the next morning.

'Have you seen Drew?' she asked Edwina with a show of studied indifference.

'No,' replied Edwina, gulping down the last of her tea and shrugging herself into her white coat.

'Oh, I'll have to give him a call, then.'

Trying to look and sound just as casual, Edwina asked, 'Are you two an item?'

For a moment, her receptionist looked troubled. 'Well, not exactly, to be honest, but it's not for want of my trying.' She gave a false laugh. 'I thought we were getting along fine, but lately . . . '

She shook her head and frowned. In the silence, Edwina asked another personal question. 'What happened with your marriage?'

Trish poured herself a second mug of coffee, and, nursing it, propped herself up against the kitchen bench.

'It's about Melanie, really. I don't want her to have the kind of life I had, wrong side of the tracks and all that. My father was a railway ganger and there never was enough money.'

'Max was a lovely bloke, and a good father, but I knew he'd never amount to much. Has no drive. He'd never be able to give Melanie the advantages that money brings, like a good education, mixing with the right people. By the time she was born I could see this and decided to divorce him.'

Edwina was astounded. 'You decided to divorce him? Isn't being a divorced, single mother a recipe for financial disaster?'

'Yes, but I figure it'll give me a chance to re-marry.'

'And Drew Colville is that chance?'

Trish nodded. 'He's very well off.' She gave Edwina a wide grin. 'And he's not a bad sort, is he?'

Edwina had never encountered such blatant scheming. At medical school there had been the usual girl-talk of marrying a doctor for his future earnings and social standing, but this divorce had been an enormous gamble.

'But, Trish, was your background so terrible? This is a lovely town — ' Edwina stopped. How could she say that? It wasn't a lovely town! Not beneath the surface. She could understand how a mother would be concerned about her daughter's future.

She thought of Melanie and all the other children of the town. And of the unlovely, uncooperative DS Walsh who didn't want to know about a possible marijuana plantation.

I'm not going to leave before I find it, she vowed. For all the kids' sakes.

7

The foyer of the hospital was unusually busy when Maureen Sweeny and Edwina passed through at the end of the rounds the next morning. Along with the bustle of newly-discharged patients and their relatives, a group of formally dressed men had gathered outside the board room, Drew among them. It was the first time Edwina had seen him since confiding in him about Timothy.

And the first time since her visit to the police station. She wondered did he know about that yet? It was hard to read his body language from a distance, if indeed there would be an outward show of that knowledge.

'There's a Board meeting this morning,' explained the director of nursing as they reached her door. 'Looks like someone is late. Why don't you wait in my office?'

111

'Wait? What for? Board meetings have nothing to do with me.'

'I've heard they want to farewell you officially.'

Edwina wasn't sure she could handle the hypocrisy of Drew, in his role of chairman, making a speech of thanks, and farewell. His silence had already said it all; her brother had been schizophrenic and he didn't want to know her.

Was it possible to flee, claiming an urgent case? As she hesitated, the overweight, plain-clothes detective shambled through the main door and joined the group. She sucked in her breath. If Drew didn't already know about her encounter with DS Walsh he soon would.

Questions crowded her brain. What was the man doing here? Was this some vindictive move on his part to report her to the board for rudeness? But what could he gain from that? She didn't pose a threat to anyone in the town; she was leaving next week.

One thing was certain — she didn't want to face him either.

'I'll take you up on your offer, Maureen,' she said, moving quickly to open the office door and slip inside. The director of nursing looked surprised at her sudden change of direction but followed her.

'I'll ask the girls in the kitchen to bring us a cuppa,' she said, lifting the phone.

Edwina shook her head and asked the question that was uppermost in her mind.

'What is that detective doing here?'

'He's on the board, but because he's only in town for the Magistrates' Court, they schedule their meetings to fit in with court sittings,' Maureen said, replacing the phone.

So there was a legitimate reason for the policeman being in the hospital. Edwina wondered if that would account for Myrtle's claim that Drew and DS Walsh had been seen together of late?

'Will you make my apologies, please,

Maureen? I'd forgotten I promised to make a house-call before lunch.' She turned with her hand on the doorknob and flashed a smile back at the non-plussed director of nursing. 'Thanks.'

Edwina wasn't surprised when Drew came through the door at the end of evening surgery. She knew making an excuse and avoiding the Board meeting earlier in the day had only postponed the inevitable. There had to be a goodbye of some sort, but at least this would be in private, without the need for pretence.

The sheaf of flowers he carried made it obvious this was an official call. Without any preamble he began what sounded like a well-rehearsed speech.

'Edwina, the Board regrets the missed opportunity to formally express their thanks for the excellent way in which you have fulfilled your contract,' he began.

She prepared herself for the goodbye-and-good-luck-in-the-future part. It shouldn't be hard for him to say, she reasoned; he probably wished her gone already. She reached out to take the floral offering and make it easier for him, but he made no effort to pass it over. Almost as if he'd forgotten he was holding anything.

'The Board has been considering the possibility of making the work-load for its doctor lighter.'

There was no doubt Dr Bill would agree with the board on that subject; the weeks spent relieving him had given her an idea of the demands of his practice. She wondered how they intended to do that. Nothing had changed, but she now knew the dark secret that explained the reluctance of doctors to come to the town.

'Dr Bill has been with us so many years we have been guilty of taking him for granted,' Drew went on.

Edwina asked herself how much longer his little prepared speech would continue before he gave up the flowers and left, duty done. And how much longer she could stand in the hallway with a pleasant smile on her face.

'The flowers . . . ?' she prompted.

Ready to take them, she moved a little closer, so close she could see his white-knuckled grip. Astonished, she realised he was nervous!

But Drew wasn't finished. 'With that in mind, the board has decided to offer you a position as assistant to Dr Bill.'

It wasn't what Edwina had expected. 'Position? Assistant?' The flowers forgotten, she half-turned away to hide her confusion. Already the questions were queuing up. Why was he nervous about asking her to stay on? Did it mean he didn't like the board's decision?

He had no need to worry on that score — she couldn't get away soon enough. Her unhappiness wouldn't last for long in new surroundings, she knew that. The strategy had worked for her coming to Australia from London. It would work again, in reverse.

With nothing to lose, she turned to face him. 'Do you agree with this?' she asked bluntly.

'Yes, of course. Why wouldn't I?'

'It's a little while since I last saw you,' she said. And told you about my brother being a schizophrenic, she could have added.

Suddenly, the flowers were in her hands. All signs of nervousness disappeared in a rush of words. 'Yes, and I'm sorry about that. I've been running around, talking with individual board members to organise a done-deal before the meeting. As it happens, I needn't have bothered — they were of one mind without any lobbying by me.'

Edwina didn't know which part of what Drew was saying to deal with first. 'Even the policeman?'

'Yes, why not?'

'Didn't he tell you I'd been to the station?'

'Yes.'

'And you didn't mind?'

'I wish you hadn't, but . . . ' He shrugged. 'You have your reasons . . . although I can't imagine what they are.'

She remembered the newspaper

editor's remark that Drew would be worried for her safety. He was wrong. But did that make Myrtle right?

If Drew and the policeman were involved in some secret activity, they should be glad to see her gone. It would seem they weren't so maybe Myrtle was wrong, too.

Edwina didn't know what to think. 'I'll put these in water,' she said, removing the cellophane from the flowers as she moved toward the kitchen. Drew followed. She decided it was as good a time as any to try for answers to awkward questions.

'Are you and DS Walsh friends?' she asked over her shoulder as she searched the cupboards for a vase.

'We are on the board.'

'Nothing other than that? I've heard you're more than friends, that you're partners . . .'

'Partners? In what?' He sounded genuinely puzzled.

Edwina suddenly saw the trap she'd set up for herself. There was only one answer to that — partners in crime. Could she make that accusation? Drew came to stand beside her at the sink, forcing her to look into his glowering face. 'What exactly are you driving at?' he demanded, his voice suddenly harsh. Her fingers stiffened, snapping the stem of the flower she was holding.

'Oh, I'm sorry, I shouldn't have said that. It's just that . . . ' She wished she could take back what she'd said and searched desperately for some way out. There was none.

'No, you shouldn't have said that,' the cold, hard voice went on. 'If you have doubts about me and any member of the board, you are free to reject the offer of a further contract. And leave.'

Edwina was aghast! Driven by feelings of rejection, she had listened to what could only be called town gossip and acted on it. She knew Myrtle meant well, wanting only to save her from heartache, but there was no excuse for her own behaviour.

In her confusion, and against her

training and long-held principles, emotion had over-ruled good sense.

Feeling guilty, she became defensive, turning the attack back on Drew.

'Well, I certainly wouldn't care to stay on and be shouted at,' she said. 'That's all you've ever done since I came here. I can't seem to do anything right where you're concerned. Why are you so angry at me?'

She didn't wait for an answer. The way she saw it, there probably wasn't one. The flowers arranged to her satisfaction, she took the vase into the hallway and set it on the receptionist's desk with a thud.

That done, she returned to the kitchen and began preparing her supper, not looking at him, trying to pretend he wasn't there.

It didn't work. Drew seemed to be everywhere she turned.

'Edwina.' There was no avoiding the tall figure planted firmly in front of her. 'Why are we doing this? What has happened between us? I thought we'd established a rapport . . . ' He took the egg-basket out of her hands and put it down on the table.

Reminded of their wonderful day together at Island Bend and its aftermath, her hurt became an avalanche of words, sweeping away all restraint. 'You talk about the rapport between us. I believed there was something there, too, but the moment I told you about my brother, whatever it was disappeared. And so did you.'

'Disappeared? No Edwina, I was — '

'You were shocked? By schizophrenia? Or by my secret? Well, how about this for a shocking secret? My brother committed suicide!'

Drew stepped up close and, before she realised his intention, enveloped her in his arms.

'Oh, Edwina, I'm so sorry,' he said into her hair. 'It must have been awful to have to bear it on your own.'

The compassion in his voice broke through her resentment. The man who, moments before, had been the focal point of her anger, became her safe harbour. She burrowed into the comfort of his embrace as the past and all its sadness became the present.

From somewhere deep down inside her came wrenching sobs that shook her whole body.

'He was alone,' she moaned. 'I wanted to be there for him . . . but there wasn't . . .' The tears were coming fast, trickling unchecked down her cheeks, hot and salty in the corners of her mouth. 'There wasn't anything . . . anyone . . . could do . . . he was lost in another world,' she explained between hiccupping sobs.

'You can't take the responsibility for the choice he made.'

'No, I know. He was beyond reach, but he was alone. That was what was so terrible.'

'And weren't you?'

Edwina leaned back in his arms and stared at Drew in astonishment. He had recognised her innermost sorrow, her long-buried loneliness.

'So you had to carry this all by

yourself? Wasn't there anyone for you at the time?' He produced a handkerchief.

Edwina allowed her wet face to be wiped then asked a question of her own. 'You aren't ... put off by schizophrenia? You don't think it hereditary?'

'Hereditary? Of course not!'

'Someone else thought so. My fiancé ... and his family.'

Drew's face told her of his dismay. 'This gets worse,' he muttered. 'What kind of people would do that?' He didn't wait for an answer, but pulled out a chair. 'Here, sit down and tell me all about it.' His gentle hands on her shoulders eased her into it.

'There isn't much to add. When Timothy was diagnosed Simon's family thought it might be hereditary and he went along with them. But you're right, it wasn't. Isn't.'

'Tim began smoking marijuana at uni and this triggered the psychosis. I don't know if Simon ever heard about what happened later, but I imagine if

Tim's illness freaked them out, his suicide would — ' Edwina broke off, unable to end the sentence. It didn't matter — they were not worth talking about.

Drew, who had been pacing the kitchen, stopped short. 'Marijuana can cause schizophrenia?'

'Yes, it's considered a contributing factor in certain people.'

'And this is why you're so keen to report what I suspect is a marijuana plantation to the police?' He came and knelt down beside her, taking her hands in his. 'Oh, Edwina, why didn't you tell me? As far as I was concerned you were meddling in something you knew nothing about, and all I could think of was the danger to you!'

'I couldn't tell you, not even when I learned the town's secret — his suicide was my secret.'

He squeezed her hands before standing up. 'Talking of secrets, we'll have to see if we can find this secret marijuana farm of yours, won't we?'

'You'd do that when you'd obviously rather not?'

'Of course. I'd be happy to, because it means so much to you. But you would probably think that, as the chairman of the hospital board, I'd have a hidden agenda, and you'd be right. In fact, I'd be willing to look into any other secret wishes you might have, to make our offer for you to stay the more attractive.'

Attractive? As Drew stood looking down at her, laughter lines crinkling his face, Edwina knew he was unaware of what made the offer too attractive for her to accept. That was one secret she wouldn't dream of confiding.

She had fallen in love with him.

8

From where she sat in the parked Land Rover, Edwina could see the approaching bank of dark clouds. It had thickened from a mere smudge on the horizon half-an-hour ago into something more threatening, almost as if a storm might be blowing up.

That was what was extraordinary about Australia. It was so different to the dull-grey London winter she'd left behind. She recalled being driven along this road on that first day, all her senses alive to the unfamiliar countryside, overawed by the space and light.

Now the vastness, the vivid colours, the heat and dust had almost become part of her. She knew it was not only Drew she would miss back in England, for going back was what she'd decided to do, despite the Board's offer of indefinite employment.

She steered her mind away from the fast-approaching departure day back to the here-and-now. Where was Drew? She glanced at her wristwatch and realised it was the second time she'd done that in the last five minutes.

This sign of her nervousness didn't surprise Edwina. There was so much hanging on the outcome of the day. What would they discover down the road that was little more than a track? An impoverished farm as she'd thought, or an illegal marijuana plantation as Drew suggested.

Of course, they might find nothing at all, making it a waste of Drew's time, compounding DS Walsh's opinion of women and their place in the scheme of things. Was it too much to hope Drew hadn't told the policeman what they planned to do?

Edwina shook her head as if to clear her mind of all the unanswerable questions. She would have to wait and see. Restlessly, she left the vehicle and wandered along the dry verge of the road.

The wind, blowing strongly since early morning, had strengthened with the afternoon heat. It tore strips of bark from the overhanging trees and dislodged twigs to fall on her.

Her hair became a tangled mess and behind the sun-glasses she wore, her eyes were gritting with dust.

Defeated by the conditions, she climbed back into the comfort of the Land Rover.

A flash of reflection on window-glass alerted her to an approaching vehicle. It was Drew. He swung in and parked in the shade, well off the road. Her eyes rested on the familiar figure as he walked the short distance between them.

Edwina found it impossible not to be affected by the sight of him, impossible to quell the lift of her heart, the quickening of her pulse.

There was no question, she had to leave. 'Sorry I'm running a little behind schedule,' he said, bending his height to greet her through the window as he grasped the door handle. 'There's bushfire in the forest near Emu Point. We've sent the Island Bend fire-fighting unit.'

'A bushfire?' Edwina peered out at the sky. The threatening storm-clouds had become smoke-clouds, billowing black and orange, shafted from behind by the sun's rays.

She clambered across into the passenger seat to allow Drew behind the steering wheel of the Land Rover. 'Should we be going now, Drew?' she asked.

'In a way, this could work in our favour. There'll be lots of to-ing and froing of fire-fighters on the road and in the forest. We won't arouse any suspicions.'

'You still think we're dealing with growers, don't you?'

He nodded. 'In my book, they're guilty until proven innocent. Not exactly Westminster justice, but we've learned to err on the safe side around here.'

'What I can't understand is why the police won't do anything about them. Walsh fobbed me off by saying he'd taken up the matter with you. He didn't, did he?'

'No, he just said you'd been to the station. Maybe he didn't want to face that it may be starting over again.'

'Have you ever thought this head-in-the-sand attitude might give the townspeople the impression of corruption?'

'PJ corrupt? You've got to be joking — he's too lazy.'

Drew stared at her, the laugh dying as comprehension took over his face. 'So that's what all the questions are about. Are you saying you thought that of me, too?'

'Some of the townspeople do,' she defended herself.

His expression became determined. 'Well, we'll just have to prove them wrong, won't we?'

'But what about the bushfire?' Edwina asked with a casualness that

130

belied her uneasiness.

'The weather bureau is expecting a change of wind direction about nightfall. That'll turn the fire back on itself. We'll be into the forest and out again long before that. Trust me, Edwina, I wouldn't knowingly put you at risk.'

He put out a hand to lightly touch her knee. The attraction she felt that kept her on the tip-toe of expectation, set all her nerve-ends quivering.

'At least I can be sure of that,' she teased to cover her pleasure at his touch. 'After all, you still need a doctor for a few more days.'

For a moment, Drew looked quite startled, then threw back his head. 'Good one, Edwina. I do have to take special care of you.' Still laughing, he engaged the gears and the vehicle began to move over the uneven ground and through the table-drain on to the asphalt. 'Now, where is this road that isn't a road?'

Edwina picked up the hand-drawn map that lay on the dashboard. 'I've written down as much as I can remember of my route that day,' she said, waving her hand to indicate the direction he should take. 'And the fuel tank is full.'

The reference to the cause of her losing her way in the first place, making this reconnaissance necessary, went unnoticed.

'Good girl,' he said.

Good girl! Was that all he could say? It had taken her hours of driving and false hopes before she found her bearing.

She could see Drew was right about the traffic on the main road. Water tankers and trucks equipped for fire-fighting passed them in increasing numbers, hurrying in the same direction as they were.

'Did you tell detective Sergeant Walsh you were meeting me out here today?'

He shot her a quizzical glance. 'No, why should I?'

'You haven't arranged for reinforcements, then?'

That amused Drew. 'The first thing PJ would ask for before venturing from his office would be evidence, so this is merely an evidence-gathering exercise.'

Edwina was glad to hear it. At least the detective wouldn't be around if the whole thing turned out to be a colossal waste of time. She couldn't bear the man's scorn.

Remnants of his smile lingered on Drew's lips.

'What? What is it?' she asked. 'Did he say something to you?'

'What makes you think I've been talking to him? I hardly ever see him.'

'You're friends with him, aren't you?'

'Not likely! You seem fixated on that idea. Who put it into your head?'

Myrtle Thompson, that's who. Not for the first time, Edwina wondered, could her patient have been wrong about other things, too? The more she learned about Drew, the more unlikely the whispers against him seemed.

Edwina began to feel uneasy. Did he suspect she'd been listening to gossip?

Did he expect her to admit how wrong it had been to take notice of it? She couldn't.

'You know, pride is a funny thing,' he mused, breaking the silence, almost as if he could read her mind. 'It's sheer pride won't let me admit I was wrong about you. I thought you were just another girl, easily forgotten. I'll miss you when you're gone, Edwina Gorton.'

A flush of pleasure warmed her face, but she had her pride, too. She wasn't going to make more of his comments than he intended. 'And I shall miss you all, too,' she responded, keeping her tone light.

Drew went on, as if he hadn't heard her. 'My mother tells me you don't realise how much you care for someone until you lose them. I think she's right. In fact, I'm sure she's right.'

He turned toward her, reached out and covered her hand with his.

'Drew, the turn-off!' The hand was withdrawn quickly and returned to the steering-wheel.

'Well, it certainly is a turn-off. Talk about bad timing! Just when I want to tell you I think I've fallen in love with you, we arrive.'

Beside him, Edwina sat very still, shocked. She couldn't believe what she'd just heard. Drew talking about love? To her? What about Trish?

He was right about one thing — this wasn't the time or place for a discussion about even hypothetical personal relationships.

She had to make herself forget. Whatever he'd said, Drew needed his whole attention to be concentrated on the track ahead.

He braked gently and pulled over to the side of the road. 'This is the so-called dead-end, isn't it?'

He waited for another fire-truck to pass before backing up and making a right-hand turn off the highway on to the less-travelled side road.

9

In the forest, smoke made visibility a problem. Edwina couldn't be sure she recognised anything familiar. She lowered the window for a better look. The wind was still gusting strongly, bending the bushes beside the track almost double and throwing debris up in front of them to crack against the windscreen glass. Instinctively, she recoiled and closed it out.

Crawling along in low gear between the stands of ghostly trees was eerie. The pungent smell of burning eucalyptus carried on the wind stayed in the cabin even after the window was closed.

'Are we getting close?' Drew asked. She nodded. The track had all but petered out and the going, even for the Land Rover, had become rough. She remembered it was here she'd had to abandon the vehicle and go seeking help.

He nosed the Land Rover out of the ruts and deep into the undergrowth and extinguished the parking lights.

Outside, the wild wind, the smell of smoke and threat of danger. Inside, the two of them together in a very strange, private world. Expectantly, she shifted her body to face him.

'I think we should be a little cautious about how we proceed from here on in,' he said.

Was he referring to his relationship with Trish? His hand was on the door-handle. 'I'll see what's up ahead. You stay here. Don't leave the vehicle.'

Edwina realised how wrong she'd been, reading too much into his words. She'd forgotten how often men flattered women with jokey comments that meant little. But she could tell Drew wasn't joking about his warning not to leave the vehicle.

Her feeling of utter foolishness was smothered by rising fear. 'What do you mean? What about the fire?'

'Relax, it's a long way off. I'm just

telling you because you've had no experience of bush-fires. Radiant heat is what kills, so it's safer to stay in a vehicle.'

Fire, radiant heat, kills, all horror words. Edwina would prefer words of flattery, however lightly bandied about. She opened her suddenly-dry mouth to protest against being left behind.

'OK, OK, simmer down. You're going to turn all doggedly-British on me, aren't you? I should've known better than to suggest it.'

He reached to touch the back of her head and drew her close. 'I don't want to leave you either, but I felt I should give you the option.' His kiss was light on her forehead. 'Let's go!'

He opened the door on his side. The burning air rushed in and then was slammed out. Edwina quailed at its strength. Suddenly the safety of the cool cabin seemed very desirable, but only for a moment. They were in this together and together they would be.

She tumbled out of the door to meet

the shadowy figure crossing in front of the vehicle.

'I thought you said we weren't in danger,' she quipped, to cover her trepidation.

'Did I say that? It must have been a slip of the tongue.' The wind threw his laugh back at her.

'That doesn't make me feel any better,' she said, half in jest, half-seriously.

Drew took her hand. 'I'll look after you,' he said and led the way through the undergrowth into the forest.

Although there was still a while to sun-down, the heavy clouds of smoke had already blocked out much of the light. In amongst the trees the darkness seemed impenetrable.

The forest floor was tinder dry and brittle under their feet, and the leaves brushed in passing felt dehydrated and almost crisp to the touch.

Longing for the coolness of just a single-top, Edwina began to peel off her cotton over-shirt.

'No, no, don't do that,' Drew shouted above the noise of the wind. 'Leave it on for protection.'

Of course. She had forgotten radiant heat. She wasn't to have even the relief of folded-back sleeves as they pushed through the bushes in the suffocating gloom.

The wind was whistling and whining through the trees, whipping the canopy above them into a frenzy of thrashing branches. Edwina felt, rather than heard, Drew's exclamation. He let go of her hand and bounded ahead.

'Wait, Drew! I'll be lost in the dark,' she called out, stumbling after him.

'Down!' he ordered quietly, but urgently as she tripped and fell over his crouched figure. He reached out and pulled her tight against his body.

'I'm sorry, I didn't mean to leave you behind, but I got carried away. Look! Your shed!'

10

Edwina blinked rapidly several times to clear her smoke-filled eyes and peered through the bushes. By now, visibility had been reduced even farther, but she recognised the green farm shed.

The relief and excitement of their find faded almost immediately. To her mind, the building looked no different to any other farm shed being used for legitimate farming practices.

That meant this dangerous trip had been for nothing.

'There's no sign of a plantation, is there, Drew?'

'And there's no sign of any farm machinery or animals, either. That is because no-one farms in the State Forest. And that is no ordinary shed. For one thing, we don't usually paint our out-buildings, especially not the roof.'

'No, I think they could be growing marijuana hydroponically in there, although from here I can't see their water supply. It's still a way to the river.'

'Hydroponically?'

'Growing plants without soil, just water and nutrients.'

'Why would they be doing that? You're not going to try and tell me there's a shortage of land, are you?'

'I think it's probably being done to avoid aerial surveillance. Planes make regular sweeps along the river during the growing season. You can see a lot from up there.'

Edwina could feel the beginnings of a coughing fit. 'You couldn't today, Drew. The smoke is getting thicker,' she wheezed.

'We'd better get on then, while we can still see.'

'This is not the way back, Drew,' she protested, trailing behind him.

'I want to find the water supply,' he called over his shoulder.

'Wait!' she begged between gasps.

He turned back, immediately concerned. 'Are you all right?' he asked, putting an arm around her shoulders and peering into her face. 'I'm sorry, I'm leaving you behind again. I don't mean to but your friend, the lazy PJ Walsh, will want evidence. Just telling him there's a shed in the forest won't be enough.' He gave her a winning smile.

'My friend!' she retorted with all the scorn she was capable of before being won over. 'All right, if you think there is evidence, but slowly, please. I'm having difficulty breathing.'

'Are you sure you're OK?' Drew's face was worried. Edwina nodded. 'Fair dinkum? We can't have anything happening to you, can we?'

For a drawn-out moment he gazed at her, his eyes seeking reassurance. Now it was no longer the smoke-filled air that was putting a strain on her breathing; her heart was racing.

He broke the spell with a laugh. 'Mustn't forget the town doesn't have a spare doctor. Well, not yet, anyway.'

His remark put paid to the foolish dream she'd allowed herself since the beginning of their search. He didn't care for her, only his hospital, and she'd been wrong to imagine there was something special going on between them. Nothing had changed; staying in Australia was not an option.

But now wasn't the time to think about the future. There was a job to do, and that meant checking out Drew's theory. It was what they'd come for.

Satisfied about her well-being, Drew turned and, leading the way, strode through the knee-high dry grass that surrounded the corrugated-iron shed. Soon, Edwina was struggling to keep up with him.

'They weren't very fire-conscious, that's for sure,' he called back over his shoulder. 'Obviously more worried about surveillance. Guess they planned on getting the crop out before the fire-season began.'

Drew followed the wall of the building, kicking at the grass, until he stopped short with a triumphant shout. Edwina wished Myrtle could see his enthusiasm. This man was in no way involved in the growing of illegal drugs here, or anywhere else.

The long grass camouflaged the outlet pipes. 'The pump will be down by the river,' Drew explained once she'd caught up. 'Let's go!'

She couldn't see why they needed to look any more, they had the evidence the detective would need to do something about the marijuana. It satisfied her.

'Drew! Stop! We shouldn't go any further. We've got what we wanted and it's getting worse.'

He stopped to gauge the worsening conditions. 'You're right, it is bad. I hadn't noticed.' He took her hand. 'Edwina, I think we should still make for the river. We'll be safer there.'

'Safer?'

'Yes, obviously the weather-front has been delayed, and the wind has strengthened. The fire could be closer than I think.'

There was an urgency to his words that hadn't been there before.

'It's always a mistake to try and out-run a fire. We'd never make the vehicle and we can't get into the shed for shelter, so it's the river. It can't be much farther.'

★   ★   ★

Edwina stood at the big window of the hospital ward, her attention caught by a rainbow flock of parrots that swooped noisily across the clear sky between the tall flowering trees in the spacious grounds.

Behind her, reflected in the glass, Drew sat propped up in bed, his dark good looks contrasting sharply with the stark white of the supporting pillows and the bandages that strapped his shoulder and upper body.

She still couldn't bring herself to like the visitor spread over a chair by the bedside. There was a lack of feeling in the beady eyes whenever they met hers.

11

This morning there had been something close to reluctant respect in his manner when he took her statement, but she found it hard to forgive him for his patronising treatment when she first sought police help.

'Everything fixed then?' DS Walsh asked Drew.

'Yup. It was bad enough tripping over their booby trap at the pump and rolling down the bank into the river, but hitting a tree and dislocating my shoulder on the way, well . . . Luckily I took my doctor with me. You should never travel without one, I say.'

Drew was making a joke of it now, but Edwina knew of the nightmare struggle to get them both out of the water to safety once the fire had roared past them. And of the anxious drive to the hospital after they'd staggered exhausted into the arms of the men from the Rural Bush Fire Brigade.

It was only then that he allowed the pain to show through the grime, his hand gripping hers, not letting go until they reached the hospital and she could treat him.

'So, all's well that ends well, eh?' pronounced the detective, without acknowledging her part in the satisfactory outcome.

She frowned at the trite saying. As if a dislocated shoulder and broken ribs could be called ending well!

Drew was remarkably good-natured in his reply. 'You could say that,' he said.

'I suppose you'll want to be in the hunt to find the perpetrators?'

'Not really, PJ. It's history as far as we're concerned, eh, Edwina? Our detective days are over. We'll leave you police to get on with whatever you have to do to get your man, or men, in this case.'

'The only part I liked was being rescued by the beautiful princess.'

149

That made Edwina laugh and turn away from the window. 'Even if the beautiful princess was a silly English twit and caused you all the trouble by getting lost in the first place and stumbling on a secret?'

He smiled across the distance between them. 'Even if,' he teased.

She believed him.

The big man coughed and squirmed in his chair, bringing attention back to what he would probably call the matter in hand.

'I'm glad you're not contemplating a career in the force. Neither of you were very good at it, getting yourself in such a fix. It was an extreme fire-danger day, after all.'

He shook his head in disbelief. 'But that's OK,' he went on pompously, turning to Edwina at last. 'You can go back to England. You won't even have to give evidence at the trial.'

Drew cut in sharply. 'The trial? You've caught them already?'

A smirk appeared on the detective's

face. 'I knew that would make you sit up and take notice. It was pretty straightforward, really.' He paused for effect.

'I began enquiries when the good doctor reported the vandalism. There were some new people in town, so we put them under surveillance . . . Tracked their delivery route, notified the Drugs Squad, and Bob's your uncle.'

One part of Edwina's mind registered that the smirk had widened into a self-satisfied smile. He was carrying one-upmanship to the extreme, enjoying every moment of his triumph.

She turned her back; she didn't want the man to see how much his behaviour affected her. It was no joking matter for her.

But some of her anger was directed against the chauvinistic detective. He could have given her some indication that he'd taken action on her complaint. It would have saved Drew and her risking their lives to get evidence he didn't need.

With an effort, the detective got up and, moving awkwardly in the narrow space between the beds, took Drew's hand and shook it. 'I don't suppose we'll be seeing much of each other from now on. It's back to the city for me.' With a fleeting sidelong glance at Edwina, he added, 'You're a lucky man, Drew Colville.'

He lumbered across the ward and out the door.

'It was a bit of a back-hander, but that's the closest you'll get to a compliment from the guy,' Drew said.

A twinge of sympathy surprised Edwina. 'You know, I'm just a little bit sorry for him. It must be awful being so unlovable.'

'Detectives don't often win popularity polls, even out here in the Bush.'

'He certainly wouldn't with women; he has a bad attitude. Did you notice how he was positively gloating at being able to bring us . . . well, no, bring me, a woman, the news of his success in tracking the culprits? The message was clear enough — men succeed!'

There was one last glimpse of the detective as he reached the hospital car-park and squeezed himself into the police car. Edwina turned away from the window and faced Drew.

'Thanks to that repulsive man, all the *i*'s have been dotted, all the *t*'s crossed — '

'Not as far as I'm concerned,' Drew interrupted. He was not smiling. 'There's something still outstanding.'

With an effort, he shifted in the bed. 'You know, I think PJ has the right idea. We sensitive, new-age guys are too soft. Well, that will have to change. Come over here!' he commanded.

12

Edwina was puzzled. What was he saying? Did he really agree with the policeman's attitude and want to boss her now they were alone? 'I've told you how I feel about you, but you haven't reciprocated,' he said, sternly.

Oh, so that was it. She stepped up to the end of bed and began to explain. 'The last twenty-four hours have scarcely been — '

'There hasn't been one word from you about how you feel. I haven't a clue,' he went on, as if unmindful of her protest. 'Although I thought I heard someone calling me darling at one stage . . . '

He was pushing the agenda ahead of Edwina's plans. This still wasn't the time or the place. He'd made what could have been a declaration of love, but it had been crowded out by the terrible day in the forest that had brought them so close to being caught in a bush-fire.

She wanted him to repeat it, but in a more romantic place. Perhaps in Island Bend's heavily-scented garden on a still night, the sky above them thick with the everlasting stars? Yes, she decided, she'd like that. When the time was right. Not now.

Still a little surprised by the change in Drew, Edwina said nothing, staring back at him, calling his bluff.

But, as the moment stretched to a minute, it was she who gave way. Something about his downcast face made the doctor in her wonder if his injury was causing him pain, if he needed further medication.

She moved closer and searched his face. A tell-tale tug was pulling at the corner of his mouth; it gave him away. He was teasing her! Well, two could play at that game.

'I don't believe this! The confident Drew Colville admitting to doubt? I thought you knew everything. You always act so knowing.'

He looked a little self-conscious. 'Falling in love makes you unsure.'

'Tell me about it,' she said with a wry grin, remembering her own uncertainties as she struggled with her growing attraction to him.

13

'You think you know a lot about women until you fall in love, then the doubting begins.'

Edwina wasn't going to take him seriously.

'So that's how you know whether or not it's love? By feeling uncertain?' she mocked. 'Oh, come on! A bit unscientific, I'd say.'

'Are you telling me this is one-sided?'

'No, no,' she came in quickly, dismayed by the stricken look on his face. The time for teasing was over.

Edwina spelt out what she thought he already knew, just in case there was any lingering doubt.

'When I met you I really wasn't interested in you or any man. You were always so short-tempered with me I was sure you disliked me, anyway. And then there was Trish ... I told myself it

157

didn't matter, my stay was going to be short-lived.'

'When the Board asked me to accept something more permanent, I realised I'd begun to care for you. But because you'd always shouted at me . . . '

Drew's face was still serious. 'You couldn't seem to understand the danger you were in. I was fearful for you, and I was right.'

'And I didn't trust you enough to tell you why I needed to do something about the marijuana.'

'Just as well you did do something. You helped the police with their enquiries, as PJ would say.'

To Edwina, they seemed to have gotten right off the subject.

'That day we spent at Island Bend I really felt you and I understood each other, but . . . '

She could see Drew was no longer listening. He seemed uncomfortable, moving restlessly, changing his position in the pillows.

'I wonder could I ask you to pull the

158

curtains around the bed? I want to do something private.'

'Shall I call someone?' she enquired, looking down the ward to the unattended nurses' station. 'They must be on their break. You'll need to press your call button.' She reached over to do it for him.

His good arm snaked around her waist and caught her unawares.

'Oh, you mean that kind of private,' she giggled, for all the world like a teenager.

She struggled awkwardly with the billowing curtain fabric and bunched-up runners, before succumbing to the insistent pressure and tumbling beside him.

'Like the man says, you're no good as a detective. You miss all the clues because you're too independent, but that's just right for what I have in mind. What do you say to a romantically-led recovery, Doctor?'

Edwina felt she should make some sort of protest before she lost her senses completely. 'Won't the nurses object?'

'To what?' he murmured into her neck.

'To me mussing up their patient. It'll get them into trouble with Maureen.'

'She may be the director of nursing, but I am the chairman of the board,' he reminded her, smothering her quibbles with his lips.

★ ★ ★

For a wounded warrior he was a good kisser, Edwina decided. Ignoring his broken ribs, she snuggled closer.

'Oh, I do love you!' It was surprisingly easy to say; the words, no longer a secret, just burst out of her as if they'd been ready for a long time. And it was easy to ask, 'Do you love me?'

She was glad she hadn't waited for a more romantic setting. His answering kiss told her all she needed to know.

'Have you any more questions, Doc?'

'No,' she gasped against his chest, for the moment, satisfied. She had to be; it

160

was a hospital. And she was his doctor.

'Good, because I have one to ask you. Will you stay and marry me?'

'That's two questions — '

'Edwina!' The confident Drew Colville was well and truly back.

After the shared horror of the bush-fire, and sure of him at last, Edwina was ready to give her heart into his keeping.

'Oh, yes,' she answered, just as confidently. She began to say more, to make certain he understood it was yes to staying and yes to marrying him.

The words were lost in his fierce embrace.

THE END